A MEMORY OF MOONLIGHT

SEA BREEZE COVE BOOK SEVEN

FIONA BAKER

D1518252

JOIN MY NEWSLETTER

If you love beachy, feel-good women's fiction, sign up to receive my newsletter, where you'll get free books, exclusive bonus content, and info on my new releases and sales!

Addison couldn't help but join in as the infectious sound rang throughout the room.

"I'm up, I'm up," Addison said, struggling to sit up and rubbing the sleep from her eyes as she brushed her blonde hair back from her face. She grabbed at Lainey, pulling her daughter into her arms and cuddling her close. "I got you!"

"Noooo!" Lainey squealed, laughing even harder and pretending to fight off her mother's snuggles, even as she cuddled closer to Addison.

"And now," Addison announced, "I'm going to eat you! Nom nom nom." She made a big show of pretending to munch on Lainey's stomach, leaving the little girl squealing with laughter.

A cry from the next room sounded, indicating that they had woken Tyler up with their antics.

"That's your brother," Addison said, gently disentangling herself from Lainey's embrace and scooting to the edge of the bed.

Lainey scrambled off the bed too, trotting after her mother to go into Tyler's room. Addison opened the door, peering through the semi-darkness to see Tyler wriggling in his crib, still howling.

"Shh, shh..." Addison cooed, walking over to him and leaning over the crib to pick him up. "Mama's got you, sweet boy."

CHAPTER ONE

Addison Foster was snuggling deeper under the covers that warded off the late-January chill in the air, savoring the warmth of her down comforter, when she felt a soft *woomp* as something small landed on the bed. Addison bit back a smile as she pretended to go back to sleep so that her daughter Lainey could have the joy of waking her up by jumping on the bed, something she liked to do every so often.

Sure enough, a moment later, the bed began wiggling as Lainey bounced around on top of the bed.

"Wake up, Mama! Wake up!" Lainey cried, bouncing even faster and giggling so hard that

Tyler's cries subsided as he realized he was safe in his mother's arms, snuggling into her embrace while Lainey danced around the two of them.

"Are you hungry, Ty?" Addison asked, kissing him on his fuzzy head. "Should we get you a bottle?"

Lainey trailed after Addison and Tyler into the living room, where Nadia was already waiting with a bottle, still looking sleepy.

Addison smiled at Nadia, touched as she always was at the way the young woman seemed to read her mind, always a step ahead and ready to help in whatever way Addison needed. The younger woman's help as a nanny and friend had been invaluable to her.

"Thank you," Addison said, taking the bottle and settling into the armchair with Tyler to feed him. Tyler instantly latched onto the bottle, nursing greedily and making Addison laugh with his soft grunts.

"Naddy, Naddy!" Lainey cried. "Wanna play with blocks?"

"You really don't have to," Addison said quietly as Lainey raced off to her room to get the toys. "It's barely even daylight. You should still be asleep."

"I don't mind," Nadia assured her, her dark

brown eyes shining. "I love your kiddos, and I was awake anyway."

Lainey returned to the living room, carrying an enormous box of brightly colored wooden blocks which she promptly dumped out on the floor before diving down to sit on Nadia's lap.

Addison continued feeding Tyler as she watched Nadia and Lainey begin building a castle together, Lainey bossing Nadia around as to how the castle needed to have two tall towers and a moat. Nadia took it all in stride, playing so sweetly with the little girl that Addison's heart swelled with gratitude and love.

Even though it was earlier than she wanted to be awake, Addison treasured these moments with her children. She loved seeing them so happy and she knew that Nadia's presence in their home was a big part of that. Even though Nadia was going through so much herself, she never let the children see it, always ready to play with a big smile and hugs galore.

As if reading her thoughts, Nadia looked up at Addison, a question in her eyes. "Is everything okay?"

Addison nodded, smiling softly. "Just thinking about how you're a true lifesaver, that's all."

"I don't know about that…"

"I do," Addison said firmly. "I don't know what we'd do without you."

"I'm just grateful to spend time with the kids, and with you. It's nice to feel like I'm part of a family."

Addison nodded, understanding how much meaning lay behind Nadia's words. Nadia's parents were going through a difficult divorce, and Addison knew that it had left the younger woman feeling adrift and unmoored. Her family was splintering, which would be painful for anyone, but Addison knew that it was especially painful for Nadia, who had been adopted. Having been given up by her birth parents, her adopted family was all she had, and now that was becoming unglued. It was enough to push anyone to the edge.

"How are you doing?" Addison asked softly, once Lainey had clambered off Nadia's lap and was fully engrossed in her castle. "I mean, how are you *really* doing?"

Nadia, whom Addison could tell had been about to brush the question off with a fake smile and a "fine," cast her eyes down, looking heartbroken.

"Things have been… really hard," she admitted,

brushing away a tear that slid down the smooth brown skin of her cheek.

"How are your parents doing?"

Nadia shrugged, toying with a block and not meeting Addison's eyes for a moment.

"Still bent on getting a divorce," she said with a bitter laugh before sighing and looking up at Addison. "I've been in touch with them a bit more, and I'm trying to come to terms with the fact that they're really going to go through with it. I think I was in denial for a while."

"Who wouldn't be? I can't even imagine what it's felt like for you."

"It's going to be okay," Nadia said, with more assurance than her face showed. Addison could tell she was trying to be a grown-up about the whole situation, and it made her heart ache for the woman even more. "I can't make this decision for them. All I can do is try to support each of them and keep on loving them the same. Anyway, I'm handling it, and it will be okay."

Addison could sense that Nadia was holding back her real feelings, trying to seem mature about a situation that was clearly tearing her apart inside. She looked at Nadia sympathetically, searching for the right words.

"You know, it's okay to not be okay in a situation like this," she said, her voice gentle. "You're allowed to feel how you feel—there's no perfect way to handle this. You don't have to be perfect in all of this and you don't have to know how to handle it all right this minute."

Addison caught sight of a glint in Nadia's eye that told her tears were rising. Nadia wiped at her eyes quickly, giving Addison a watery smile.

"Thank you," she whispered. "It's been so hard to try and keep it together all the time."

"I'm sure it has been," Addison murmured empathetically.

Jesse walked into the living room, his shaggy brown hair still wet from the shower. "How are my kiddos this fine morning?" he boomed, taking Tyler out of Addison's arms and snuggling him close.

"Papa! Papa!" Lainey cried, jumping to her feet and running over to Jesse to wrap her arms around his legs.

"Morning, bug," he said, tousling Lainey's hair. "How would you like some banana pancakes for breakfast, hmm?"

"Banana pancakes?" Lainey bellowed. "Yes! Yes! Yes!"

Jesse laughed. "I thought you might like that. Want to help me make them?"

Lainey nodded so hard her hair flipped into her eyes.

"I'll take that as a yes," Jesse said with a chuckle as he handed Tyler back to Addison. "Come on, squirt. Let's go make breakfast for everyone."

Jesse planted a kiss on Addison's forehead and smiled at Nadia before following Lainey into the kitchen, where the sounds of pans clanging and happy chatter soon followed. Addison turned back to Nadia, who was still fiddling absentmindedly with a block, her eyes sad. She reached out and touched the younger woman's arm. Nadia looked up at her, a question in her eyes.

Addison hesitated, then asked what had been on her mind for a while. "Have you given any more thought to looking for your birth parents?"

"I..." Nadia gulped, then nodded. "Yes." She set the block aside, pulling her knees up to her chest and wrapping her arms around them. "It's been on my mind quite a bit. I even told Hector about it and he said that he'd help me any way he could."

"That was kind of him."

Nadia nodded. "I still don't know if I'm going to take him up on his offer, though. For right now I'm in something of a holding pattern—just waiting until I can figure out if that's a step I really want to take."

"I can understand that. It's a big decision—definitely not one that you need to make on anyone else's timetable," Addison assured her. "That being said, maybe finding out about that part of your past would give you a feeling of closure. Who knows?"

Nadia nodded and leaned over to give Addison a hug. "Thanks for listening. I'll think about it."

"It's just a thought. I don't mean to pressure you."

"I know, and I appreciate it."

Addison let the subject drop, knowing it was difficult for Nadia to talk about it. "How about some banana pancakes? They should be almost ready by now."

"Yes, please," Nadia said, jumping to her feet. "Banana pancakes sound like just the thing right now."

Addison smiled, following the nanny into the kitchen where the delicious smell of pancakes was wafting through the room. Despite what Nadia was going through at the moment, it was good to see Nadia smiling at the sight of flour all over Lainey's cheeks.

She's going to be okay, Addison thought, putting Tyler in his high chair. *She's going to get through this.*

Sadie McCall tucked her arm through her boyfriend's as she and Ethan Gilbert walked up the path to the property at the end of the cul-de-sac.

They had finally closed on the property for their new business venture, and Sadie still couldn't quite believe that the house she was looking at belonged to her, Ethan, and Addison. Sure, the house needed more than a little work, but it had good bones, and she could already envision it in all its finished glory.

Silver, who Sadie held on a leash, sniffed around the front of the house and barked happily, which made Sadie and Ethan laugh.

"I'd say that Silver approves," Ethan said, smiling down at Sadie. "So do I, for that matter."

"I'm glad you like it." Their realtor, Hector Morales, watched them both with a satisfied expression on his face.

Just then, Ethan's cell phone rang. He looked down at the screen. "That's one of the vendors with supplies we need for the house. I need to take this."

"Go ahead," Sadie urged him, dropping his arm so he could walk away.

She turned, noticing as she did so that Hector's face had settled into lines of worry, so different from the delighted expression he'd been wearing just a moment before. She took a step toward him, speaking quietly enough that it wouldn't bother Ethan on his phone call.

"Hector? Is everything all right?"

Hector blinked, seeming to come back to the moment and finally shrugged. "I... I'm worried about Nadia," he finally admitted. "We've been spending more time together, but she's got a lot on her plate and I know it's got her really down. I just feel so helpless. I want to do something to help her out, to fix the problems she's facing, but I'm not sure where to start." He looked at Sadie. "I was able to find you and Addison this house, and I want to be able to fix things for Nadia just as easily."

Sadie considered this. "That's a sweet thought," she said slowly. "That being said, finding solutions for *people* is a bit more complicated than helping people find the right property for their needs."

"I know," Hector said, giving her a grudging smile. He sighed, running his hand through his dark hair. "It's just so frustrating to not be able to fix the problem that easily."

"Well, Nadia is lucky to have you in her corner. If you want my advice?"

Hector nodded eagerly.

"Well, in my opinion, you should let Nadia take the lead on how she wants to handle her family problems, rather than trying to fix it the way you think it needs to be fixed. Basically, the most important thing is for you to be there for Nadia, not try to fix things for her. Does that make sense?"

Hector nodded slowly, sighing again. "I know you're right. It's hard to sit back and not try to fix things, but you're right that I need to let her figure this out and just be a support to her. Thanks for the advice."

"Sorry it wasn't the easiest to take," Sadie said with a smile.

Hector's phone rang and he looked down at it, giving a small gasp. "I'm late for another showing! I've got to run. Thanks again!"

Sadie waved as he hurried down the sidewalk toward his call. Ethan stepped up to her side, tucking his phone back into his pocket.

"So, what's going on with Hector?" Ethan asked, bending down to pet Silver.

"What do you mean?"

"Well, even though I couldn't hear your conversation, it looked pretty intense."

Sadie nodded, sighing. "Just matters of the heart, that's all."

Ethan pulled Sadie into his arms, dropping a kiss on her forehead. "Well, I'm glad when it comes to matters of the heart, the two of us are happy and settled together."

Sadie smiled up at him, melting into his arms. "Me too," she agreed fervently, pressing a soft kiss to his lips. "Me too."

CHAPTER TWO

Charlotte Winters furrowed her brow, her eyes skimming over the words on her computer screen as she read a tricky sentence over and over. Finally, her brow smoothed as she figured out the perfect word to revise the sentence. She reread it to herself, murmuring the words aloud to see how they flowed and then finally sat back, pleased with her work.

It had been a long day working at the bookshop she ran, and she had come home eager to work on her own book.

She stretched back in her seat, realizing her shoulders and neck had cramped up from sitting in one position for too long as she had worked on revising her novel. Letting out a deep sigh, Charlotte tipped her head back to stare at the ceiling and rolled her neck from side to side. Despite the aches and pains of working a long day, she was pleased with the revisions she had made and was feeling satisfied with her progress.

"Well, Bruno, all in a day's work," she said to her dog, who was resting on her feet, head on his paws.

He perked up at the sound of his name, giving a soft *woof* and tilting his nose up toward her for some scratches. She complied, rubbing his snout and scratching between his ears. He stretched luxuriously, leaning into her hand, his eyes rolling back in his head. Charlotte laughed softly, bending down to kiss the top of his furry head. Bruno tilted his head to the side, studying her, then lapped at her aching fingers with his slobbery tongue.

Charlotte laughed again, wiping her hand on her sweater and rising from her seat. As she did so, her stomach rumbled with hunger, and she realized she hadn't eaten since breakfast. Already, the sky outside was darkening as nightfall approached, meaning some good food was long overdue.

Padding into the kitchen in her stocking feet, Charlotte rummaged in the fridge and the cupboards, pulling ingredients out to throw together an impromptu dinner. She began chopping some roasted red pepper and threw it on top of a bed of spinach, dolloping the top with a few teaspoons of ricotta and some red wine vinegar dressing.

Deciding that a salad wouldn't be nearly enough to take the edge off of her hunger, Charlotte pulled some chicken breasts out of the fridge. In a saucepan, she stirred up a lemon and butter sauce. Once the mixture was bubbling, she threw the chicken breasts into it, frying them up.

As she worked, the back door opened and Briggs Callahan strode through it, dirty and sweaty from a long day of work. He paused only long enough to blow her an air kiss, showing her his dirty hands and promising to return in a couple of minutes.

Charlotte could hear the sink turn on in the bathroom down the hall as Briggs began washing up. She hummed as she turned the chicken breasts over, pleased to see they were turning the perfect shade of golden brown. The aromas of the food washed over her, making her salivate and her stomach grumbled even louder.

While Briggs changed into fresh clothes, Charlotte set the table with plates and cutlery, adding a bottle of wine to the center of the table and some wine glasses. By the time she was finished setting out the food, Briggs had emerged from cleaning up, wearing a fresh shirt and looking a good deal cleaner. Briggs pulled out Charlotte's chair for her, not taking his seat until she was settled. Then he reached for her hand.

"Dinner looks delicious," he murmured, raising her hand to his lips to press a gentle kiss to her knuckles. "Thank you for making it."

"It's nothing," Charlotte assured him. "I just threw it together. It took no time at all."

"You never cease to amaze me," he replied, beginning to dish up some of the salad onto his plate. "You could've fooled me. This looks gourmet."

Charlotte laughed lightly, dishing up a chicken breast and then adding some salad to the side of her plate. Beside her, Briggs dug into the meal, wolfing it down speedily, clearly starving from a day full of manual labor. Charlotte ate quietly beside him, enjoying the harmonious flavors of the meal. Finally, Briggs finished off his last bite and sat back in his seat with a sigh of contentment.

"I just ate way too fast," he admitted with a laugh. "But it was so good I couldn't stop myself!"

"I don't mind. You work hard. Of course you come home starving."

Briggs squeezed Charlotte's hand and looked into her eyes. "You work plenty hard too, between

The Book Nook, your novel, and now the wedding. How are things coming with the wedding plans?"

"Good! I talked on the phone with Elise this morning, and it looks like she might have found a vendor to do our flowers, so that's great news."

"Awesome. Can they do the flower arch as well?"

"That's what Elise said. Plus, they're willing to cut us a deal since we're ordering so many flowers."

"Even better. That's what I like to hear."

Charlotte sat forward, searching Briggs's blue eyes. "I just want to make sure. Are you really okay with doing this double wedding with Gabe and Elise? It's your day too, and I don't want to do anything that would make you unhappy."

"A joint wedding is unconventional, I'll give you that, but I really don't mind. I'm just as close with Gabe as you are with Elise, and nothing would make me happier than to stand beside him. At the end of the day, Char, the only thing I really want is to be married to you. Sooner rather than later," he added, flashing her a smile. "Did you and Elise talk wedding dates?"

Charlotte nodded. "We're thinking about having the wedding in May. I know it doesn't give us a ton of time, but since we're keeping things simple I think it should be okay."

"May sounds good to me. What day should we do?"

"I've always wanted an early spring wedding, before it gets too hot with summer coming in. How about May twelfth?"

"May twelfth has a nice ring to it," Briggs agreed. "Confirm with Elise, but I say, let's do it."

"Sounds good to me," Charlotte said, pulling out her phone and shooting a quick text to Elise with the planned date.

Briggs took hold of Charlotte's hand again, brushing his thumb across her knuckles as he looked deeply into her eyes.

"I still can't believe that I get to marry you," he murmured, his voice low and warm. He shook his head. "After losing my wife and son, I never thought I'd be happy again, much less find love again. You've given me a whole new life, and I don't think I'll ever be able to express enough gratitude to you for that."

"I feel the same way about you," Charlotte replied, reaching out to stroke his cheek. "You're my everything, do you realize that?"

He leaned forward, capturing her lips with his own and pressing the sweetest of kisses to them. It was a while before they finally broke apart. When they did, Briggs still kept hold of Charlotte's hand.

"We'd better clean up dinner," she finally said, loath to break the moment but ready to get the kitchen cleaned up so they could snuggle on the couch.

"Aye, aye, captain," he joked, and she swatted at him.

Together they began clearing up the table, carrying the dirty dishes to the sink where Briggs rinsed them off and began loading the dishwasher. Charlotte took a damp rag and began wiping down the table and the countertops, cleaning up from the dinner preparations.

"How did revisions go today?" Briggs asked as he loaded their plates into the dishwasher.

"Really well," she said brightly. "Better than I expected."

"That's good to hear. Is Liz still in town, or did she finally go back to New York so you can write in peace?"

Charlotte shot her fiancé a look. "Liz is still in town and she'll be here for a while longer. I'm not sure when she plans to go back to New York, actually."

Briggs pulled a face. "Is she staying around to put the pressure on you to write your book the way *she* wants?"

She shook her head. "I've actually got the feeling that there's something else keeping her here. Something personal. She hasn't talked about it to me, but I've got a hunch."

"Hmm," he murmured, but that was all he said on the subject. "Well, just as long as she lets you write your book the way you want, I guess it's not a problem."

She walked over to him and wrapped her arms around his waist. "I'm holding my own, I promise," she assured him. "You don't need to worry about me."

"I'll always worry about you," Briggs said, dropping a kiss onto her forehead.

Bruno pawed at their legs, whining for table scraps, which made the two of them laugh.

"You're such a mooch," Charlotte told him, just as her phone began ringing. She pulled it from her pocket and saw that Nina was calling. She answered the phone. "Hey, sis, what's up?"

"Hey, Char. Just wanted to give you a heads up that Mom is planning to visit Sea Breeze Cove soon. I just got off the phone with her."

Charlotte blew out a breath, rubbing at her forehead. She loved her mother, but her mom's visits always brought a special stress with them. "Well, she can help with the wedding planning," she said, a little too brightly, even as she cringed at the thought of her perfectionistic mother swooping in to take control.

"Just don't let Mom take over," Nina warned, echoing Charlotte's own thoughts.

"I'll try not to," Charlotte replied, wondering already if that was even possible. She blew out a breath. "Thanks again for letting me know."

"No problem. I'll try and act as a buffer if I can."

Charlotte grinned. "Thanks. You always know just how to help out."

"I live to serve," Nina replied sassily, and they both laughed before ending the call.

Liz Porter sat propped up on her bed in her hotel room, trying to sort through her emails. Even as she tried to focus on her work, her mind kept drifting back to the picture of her daughter, Nadia Bailey. Finally, realizing she wasn't actually going to be able to get any more work done that evening, Liz clicked back over to the email from the private investigator and opened the file that contained Nadia's picture. She could see parts of herself in her daughter's face and, once again, she wondered if meeting Nadia was a good idea.

Memories from the past assailed her, tightening their grip over her attention. She swallowed hard, remembering back to the days when she was a much younger woman, new to the publishing scene in New York City and had met another up-and-coming publisher who had captured her attention with his roguish smiles and that dimple in his cheek. Liz covered her eyes with her hands, remembering his face and how quickly she had fallen for him. Never one to be a romantic, Liz had tumbled head over heels for the man, even to the point that she was envisioning marriage.

Unfortunately for her, the relationship had only been serious on one side—hers. As quickly as it had begun, it ended, with him leaving to pursue his dreams in Hollywood, leaving her to pick up the shattered pieces of her heart.

To make a heartbreaking situation even harder, Liz had found out soon after that she was pregnant. Of course, she had tried to reach out to her ex-lover, but he was nowhere to be found, leaving Liz to deal with the growing life inside of her all by herself. Unable to fathom motherhood all by herself, Liz had made the gut-wrenching decision to give her baby up for adoption.

Tears slid down Liz's cheeks as she remembered giving her baby away and the painful years that had ensued after that, always wondering about her long lost child. Well, now she didn't need to wonder where the child was—she was here, in this very town.

Was this the time to reconnect with her child?

Liz rubbed at her watery eyes, wiping away the tears and wrestling with the question that had been at the forefront of her mind since she had received the email about Nadia.

Deciding she needed to clear her head, Liz closed her laptop and changed into workout clothes, heading down to the hotel gym. As she pushed open the door to the gym, she was greeted by a handsome trainer with blonde hair and blue eyes who hurried up to her.

"Hi, I'm Andy Kaplan, I'm a trainer here at the hotel. Can I help you craft a workout?"

The last thing Liz wanted was to talk to anyone, so she quickly shook her head. "No thanks. I'm just going to run on the treadmill."

"No worries," he said, flashing her a smile that made her heart jerk a little in her chest.

Liz hurried over to the treadmill, wondering why

her heart had thudded like that at his smile and mentally scolding herself. She hopped onto the treadmill, groaning inwardly as she saw that the dashboard of the treadmill was covered in a myriad of buttons. Why did these treadmills have to be so technologically advanced? Liz prodded at a few buttons, but nothing happened. Sighing, she turned back to Andy, who was watching her.

"Actually, I might need your help," she admitted sheepishly.

"Absolutely," he said, running over to help her. "What can I do for you?"

"I just want to figure out how to turn this darn thing on," she said, twisting a lock of her dark hair around her finger. "I swear, I'm not usually this incompetent."

Andy waved that away with a laugh. "You're not incompetent. They just make these things way more complicated than they need to be. Everyone has trouble with them."

Liz laughed. "Glad I'm not the only one."

"Trust me, you're not." Andy hit a few buttons and the treadmill turned on, then he showed her how to adjust the speed and incline. "I'll be on the next treadmill getting my own workout in," he told her, "so just holler if you have any questions."

"Will do. Thanks."

Liz began her jog, highly aware of Andy running on the treadmill beside hers. Unconsciously, she upped her pace to outrun him and she noticed him doing the same thing a moment later. For the next half hour, the two raced each other on their separate treadmills, until they finally stopped, laughing and breathing hard.

"Wow, you gave me a run for my money," Andy said.

"That's the hardest I've worked in a long time," Liz said, holding a stitch in her side. "I guess you gave me a training session after all. I might collapse on the way to my room."

"Well, we can't have that." Andy chuckled. "Here, let me walk you to your room."

"You don't have to, really," Liz said, even as she hoped that he would.

"It's no trouble. I'm done for the day here anyway."

They left the gym together, walking on jelly legs to the elevator together. All too soon they were stopping in front of her room. The time had passed far too quickly for Liz's liking and she wondered once again why she was having such a reaction to this man.

"Well, this is me," Liz said, stopping outside her hotel room door.

"Well, Liz, it was nice to meet you," Andy said, reaching out to shake her hand.

Liz held back a gasp as electricity zinged up from where their hands were touching. She smiled at him, hoping he hadn't seen her reaction.

"Maybe I'll see you around," she said.

"I hope so," Andy said, stuffing his hands into his pockets and taking a step back. "Have a good night."

Back in her room, Liz leaned her back against the door, waiting for her heart to stop beating quite so hard. As she undressed and headed for the shower, her thoughts turned once again to Nadia and the questions from before all came back to her. She had to admit to herself that, despite her fears, she really wanted to get to know Nadia. The question was, what was the best way to go about that goal?

CHAPTER THREE

Nina Winters hurried down the hallway of her new apartment to answer the door when she heard Oliver's usual knock—one long tap followed by two short ones. She pulled open the door, a smile already on her face, to see her handsome boyfriend waiting on the front doormat. Before he could even say hello, she had launched herself into his arms and planted a huge kiss right on his surprised lips.

"Whoa," Oliver said when they finally broke apart. "What did I do to earn that warm welcome?"

Nina laughed, taking his hand and dragging him into her apartment. "I just missed you, that's all."

"Then I need to find a way to make you miss me more often," he teased, snagging her around the waist and going in for another kiss.

This time, though, Nina cut it short. "We have s'mores popcorn to make, good sir."

Oliver raised an eyebrow. "And this s'mores popcorn is better than kissing?" he asked, his voice incredulous.

Nina swatted at him playfully. "Trust me, once you've tried this popcorn, you'll be in total agreement."

"I'll believe that when I see it," Oliver replied, dropping a quick kiss to her lips and pretending to consider it. "No, no, I really don't think any popcorn can beat kissing you."

Nina rolled her eyes, even as her heart warmed and she laughed. "Okay, you scoundrel, let's get to work."

"Lead the way, m'lady."

Nina pulled him into the kitchen, where she had set out the popcorn maker as well as the rest of their supplies. Nina showed him how to work the popcorn maker, then set to work herself. In a few minutes, they had a huge bowl full of fluffy white popped corn kernels, which Nina drizzled with chocolate she had melted. Oliver came in after her and drizzled the mixture with marshmallow cream, then Nina added crushed graham crackers to the whole gooey mass, which they then mixed all together.

"It's not a pretty snack," Nina said, looking down at the bowl, "but it's insanely delicious. Believe me."

"Oh, I know," Oliver agreed. "I've been snagging bites when you had your back turned."

Nina hooted with laughter, swatting at him again. "You really *are* a rogue and a scoundrel."

"Only for you," he cooed, winking at her.

"Come on, let's go pick out a movie."

Oliver carried in the bowl for them, while Nina got the remote for the TV and settled in on the cushy sofa. Oliver settled beside her, slinging one of his arms around her and spreading a blanket across both of their laps. Nina opened up Netflix on the TV and soon they were browsing through a nearly endless array of possibilities, discussing the merits of various TV shows and movies.

"I heard that your mom is coming into town," Oliver commented through a mouthful of s'mores popcorn.

Nina released a small groan, setting the TV remote down for a moment and burying her face into Oliver's shoulder. "I know... don't remind me."

"Hey, it can't be that bad."

Nina lifted her face to look up at him. "Oh, yes it can. You have no idea what she can be like."

"I thought you loved your mother."

"I do," Nina insisted, then pulled a face. "We just have a better relationship from a distance. She can be... controlling. It can be a bit much."

Oliver considered this. "Well, on the bright side, she'll have Charlotte and Briggs's wedding to focus on. That should help take the spotlight off you a little bit, don't you think?"

Nina nodded. "She'll definitely want to delve into that thoroughly while she's here, but I still don't think it will stop her from sticking her nose into *our* relationship."

Oliver shrugged. "And would that be so bad? Any loving mother would want to know who you're dating and make sure he's a good guy."

"Well, yes. Mom's heart is usually in the right place and, when she *does* stick her nose into our relationship, I know it'll be because she wants to make sure I'm safe and well cared for. Which I am," she added, reaching up to plant a kiss on his cheek. "The problem is," she continued with a sigh, "she can be a bit too intense about it all. It might scare you off."

Oliver shook his head, rolling his hazel eyes. "Do you think I'm that much of a coward? Let me put it this way—a pack of wild dogs couldn't tear me away from your side."

Nina laughed in spite of herself at his cheesy joke. "I'm going to hold you to that, you know, because you might be rethinking your words after you meet my mom."

Oliver kissed her on the nose, butterfly light. "Challenge accepted," he teased, then he sobered. "Seriously, though, your mom is not going to come between us, I promise. I'm here to stay."

Nina let out a sigh of relief, then snuggled closer into Oliver's arms. "Good. Because there's no way I want to lose you now. Not when I know you can make s'mores popcorn like a pro."

"Hey!"

"Kidding, kidding... mostly," Nina added with a roguish wink.

"Let's pick a movie before I change my mind," Oliver pretended to grump.

They scrolled through dozens more options before they finally settled on a screwball comedy from the 1930s, laughing together at the silly antics on the screen as they munched on their s'mores popcorn and held hands. Although Nina was still worried about Melissa's impending visit to Sea Breeze Cove, she decided to put it out of her mind for the time being and simply enjoy this moment with her wonderful boyfriend.

* * *

"That should be the last of the paint," Sadie said, setting down a paint can next to Ethan's feet.

He was already painting the walls of their kennel, which had been in sore need of a fresh coat. Sadie and Addison had picked out a light gray that would hide scuff marks and make the place look fresh and clean. On this particular mid-February day, Addison was busy with her children, so it was just Ethan and Sadie working on the kennel, but Sadie didn't mind. She always relished the chance to spend time alone with her boyfriend.

Silver barked happily, running around the room and then down the hallway, exploring all the other rooms in the house. Sadie had thought about leaving him at home, but she had seen no reason to leave him alone all day when he could explore the new property which would, after all, be for dogs just like him. A moment later, he whizzed back into the main room of the kennel, hurrying over to where Sadie was just dipping a roller brush into the tray of paint to help Ethan. Silver, trying to help, accidentally stepped into the tray of paint and started leaving a trail of pawprints on the drop cloth.

"Silver!" Sadie cried, setting her paintbrush

down and hurrying over to clean off his paws. "The paint is not for you!"

"He's just trying to help," Ethan said with a laugh.

"I know, I know," Sadie grumbled, then sent the dog away and picked up her roller brush again.

They worked in silence for a few minutes, each lost in their own thoughts as they spread the gray paint over the walls. Sadie took a step back, taking in their progress and thought to herself that it was looking much better than it had before. She dipped her roller brush into the paint again and continued to paint. They were still working on the first room, but they still had so many rooms to paint, she sometimes wondered if they would ever be finished with the task.

Just then, Silver raced back into the room and, like clockwork, headed straight for the tray of paint, getting his paws messy once more. Sadie groaned, laughing a little in spite of herself, while she paused to clean Silver's paws up.

"Okay, that's it," she said, leading Silver to the back door. "Time for you to get some of your energy out in the backyard."

"Thank goodness for that fenced in yard," Ethan

said as Sadie opened the door and shooed Silver outside.

"No kidding," Sadie replied, watching Silver race around the backyard for a moment, barking happily. She smiled to herself. If Silver loved the yard that much, so would all the other dogs.

Sadie had just picked up her roller brush and gotten back to work when Ethan's phone chimed with an incoming email. Ethan paused in his work, fishing his phone out of his pocket to glance over the email. Sadie watched him, curiosity enveloping her as his eyes went wide while he read the message.

"Is something wrong?" Sadie asked, concern filling her.

Ethan jumped a little, looking up at her and stuffing his phone back into his pocket a little too quickly. "Not at all," he said with a grin. "In fact, I might have the best news possible for you soon."

"The best news... what are you talking about?"

Ethan shook his head. "Uh-uh, I'm not telling you a thing."

Sadie's heart began to race with excitement. What sort of surprise was her boyfriend planning? "Come on, you can give me just a little hint, can't you?"

Ethan shook his head again. "Not a word. You'll just have to wait until I know for sure."

Sadie groaned even as she couldn't help but grin. "Know what for sure?"

"Sadie..."

"All right, all right, I'll let it go," she said, turning back to paint the wall with a smile. "Even though you're not playing fair."

"Just trust me."

"You know that I do," Sadie said, and this time her voice was warm and serious. "With my whole heart."

"Good," Ethan said, leaning over to press a quick kiss to her lips. "By the way, you should probably let Silver back in. It's still pretty chilly out. Hopefully he's gotten his wiggles out."

"Good point."

Sadie went to the door and opened it, whistling for Silver. He bounded up to her, panting slightly, his tongue lolling out. "Come on inside, cutie," she cooed. "Just don't step in the paint."

Silver, his tail wagging, hurried over to Ethan, sniffing the new wall and, like clockwork, accidentally stepped one paw into the tray of paint. Sadie and Ethan both groaned simultaneously and Sadie hurried over to wipe his paw off on the drop cloth before leading him to one of the large empty rooms down the hallway.

"I'm going to shut Silver in here for a little while so he can take a nap," she called to Ethan, then closed Silver into the room. "I'll be back for you soon, baby," she said through the door. "Just wait until we're done painting."

When she got back into the front room, Ethan had already finished one of the walls. "Looking good," she commented.

"Thanks," Ethan replied, dipping his roller into the paint tray. "Now come on, slacker, these walls aren't going to paint themselves," he teased.

CHAPTER FOUR

"Have fun studying!"

Nadia turned around and waved goodbye to Addison, who was standing in the doorway, Tyler on one hip. "I'll try," she responded, giving Addison a half-smile. "I don't know that 'fun' is the word I would use to describe studying, but I'll do my best."

Addison gave her one last wave before closing the door and Nadia headed over to her small, beat-up car. She had decided to study in a downtown coffee shop for the evening, since Addison had given her the night off. Studying at Addison's place wasn't always the easiest—especially with Lainey always barging into her room, wanting to play. With spring semester now in full swing, Nadia was feeling the pressure to get on top of her ever-growing mountain of homework and studying.

Not feeling like listening to music, she made the drive into downtown Sea Breeze Cove in silence, her thoughts drifting, as they always did lately, to the situation with her parents. Felicia and Arnold were becoming more and more acrimonious with one another, and both were trying to recruit her to their side of things. Nadia hated being in the middle of the fractured family situation and she hated feeling like her parents were at war with one another.

Pulling into a parking space, Nadia grabbed her backpack and headed into the quaint downtown coffee shop. She went up to the counter and ordered a caramel macchiato and then found a table in the corner where she could spread out her study materials and hopefully work uninterrupted. A few moments later, the barista called her name and she went up to pick up her coffee, carrying it carefully back to her table. Heaving a great sigh, she pulled out her laptop and her textbook for Intro to Sociology. She had a massive paper to write for the class—far longer, she thought, than was strictly appropriate for a 100-level class.

Taking a sip of her coffee, she dived into the reading for the class, highlighting pertinent information and jotting down notes in her notebook. She had only been working for twenty minutes or so when she caught herself staring into space, her textbook and notes forgotten as her thoughts turned inexorably back to the situation with her parents. The divorce was becoming ever more contentious, something Nadia had hoped would not occur. Alas, however, her worst fears were coming true.

Dropping her head into her hands, Nadia took a few deep breaths and tried to force her thoughts back to her studies, reminding herself that she couldn't afford to fall behind in her schoolwork and she really, *really* didn't want to have to tell Addison and Jesse that she wouldn't be able to juggle nannying and her course load once more. Taking in a few more steadying breaths, she picked up her pencil and continued jotting down notes where she had left off, pausing only to take a few more sips of her coffee.

Her phone buzzed on the table beside her and she glanced at it, biting back a groan when she saw that it was a text from her mother. She didn't even bother opening up the message—she already knew that it would be some bitter complaint about her father and that her mother would try to sway her to her side. Nadia just couldn't handle it at the moment. She was still in touch with her brother, who was going through the same thing, but she had been forced to ignore more and more messages from her mom and dad. She hated to do it—it felt so hateful and cold, but she didn't know how else to handle the contentious situation that had left her family in pieces. At least she still had Samuel, though it wasn't the same as having her whole family in harmony.

Realizing she needed a break from reading and taking notes, Nadia pulled her planner from her backpack and began sorting through the upcoming exams and assignments she had, trying to schedule out her time more properly so that she could still fit in her nannying duties. It looked like she had a lot of late nights ahead of her, and she tried not to cry just thinking about how much strain she was under. Nadia picked up her coffee, holding it in both hands and taking another slow sip, trying to slow her heart rate, which was now beating faster than it should be from the stress.

The bell at the front door of the shop jingled as someone walked in. Nadia looked up to see none other than Hector entering the coffee shop. He looked around as he entered, meeting her eyes, and Nadia gave him a welcoming smile as their gazes locked. Instead of heading for the counter to order, he walked over to her.

"Mind if I pull up a chair?"

"Aren't you going to order?"

"Yup, but then can I sit with you?"

"Of course, you don't even need to ask."

Hector raised an eyebrow, looking around at her study materials scattered all over the table. "Well, you look like you're in the middle of something..."

Nadia waved that away. "I was trying to do homework, but I wasn't making much progress anyway. Trust me, I would love your company."

Hector grinned at her. "Then I'll be right back."

Nadia watched as he turned and went to the counter to place his order, then focused on clearing some space at the table for him, stacking up her textbook and notebook and shutting her laptop. A couple of minutes later, Hector had returned with his mug of coffee and had taken the seat beside her.

"So," he said, taking a sip of his coffee and giving her an appraising look. "How are things going for you?"

"School is busy."

Hector nodded, but he still had that appraising look on his face. "I'm sure it is, but that's not really what I was asking about. How are things going with your family?"

Nadia bit her lip, blinking back the sudden,

burning tears that had risen to the corners of her eyes. She could feel her lip trembling and she looked away from him. Immediately, she felt the soft pressure of his hand on hers, squeezing gently. She held onto it like it was a lifeline, not even embarrassed at the way she suddenly needed that reassurance.

"That bad, huh?" he asked, his voice soft and sympathetic.

Nadia nodded. "It's getting so much worse than I ever thought it would," she whispered, finally meeting his eyes.

"Do you want to talk about it?"

She hesitated, not sure if she could do it without crying, but then the overwhelming need to confide in someone rose up from somewhere deep within herself, and she nodded.

"Okay, tell me everything."

Nadia took a deep breath. "I was hoping that my parents would reconcile and get back together, but I can see now that that is never going to happen. So then, of course, I hoped that at least they would be civil with one another and have an amicable separation."

"And that's not happening?"

"Not even close... they fight all the time now and

they're no longer living together. They're fighting tooth and nail over who gets the house, the cars, and most of all, the loyalty of their children."

"They're trying to make you and your brother pick sides?"

Nadia nodded, reaching up to wipe at some tears that had begun to trickle from the corners of her eyes. "Yes, they are, and it's awful."

"I can't even imagine..."

"How could I be expected to pick a side? I'm not going to, but that hasn't stopped them from trying to force me and Samuel to pick a side to be loyal to. I just... I feel so off-balance these days, like I'm being torn in a thousand different directions."

"I can definitely see why you would feel that way," Hector said sympathetically, squeezing her hand. "And I'm sure trying to balance school and nannying on top of all that is no picnic."

Nadia looked at him, grateful that he understood what she was going through. "I'm falling apart, if I'm being honest with you. I feel like I'm behind in everything and I can't seem to catch up no matter what I do."

Hector hesitated, seeming to search for the right words, then finally spoke. "I don't know if this would help you or not, but have you ever considered searching for your biological parents in all of this? Maybe finding them would help you to feel more grounded, like you're still connected to a family that's whole."

"I've thought about it," Nadia admitted. "Back when my family was still in one piece, I asked my adoptive parents about finding my bio parents, but nothing came of it. I had a closed adoption and my parents never met the woman that gave birth to me, so there's not much my parents can tell me about my past."

"I see... well, if you ever wanted to keep searching for your biological parents, remember that I promised I would do whatever I could to help." He paused, then continued. "That being said, I totally understand and wouldn't blame you if you just want to let sleeping dogs lie and not look into it."

Nadia sat back in her seat, mulling over his words. There were pros and cons to both roads, and she wasn't totally sure which route was the best option. Her parents' divorce was definitely a catalyst in wanting to locate her birth mother, but as she examined her feelings she found that she really did want to find her biological mom totally apart from what was going on in her own personal life. Addison's words about finding closure returned to her and she couldn't help but think that maybe Addison and Hector were right.

"I think I do want to find my birth mom," Nadia finally said. "I can't live the rest of my life wondering about where I came from and if I find her that would be one less question rolling around in my head. I don't think I'll be able to find peace and closure *without* finding her, to be honest."

Hector nodded, his expression warm and understanding. "Well, like I said, I'll do everything in my power to help you find her. I know your adoption was closed, but sometimes it's possible for someone who was adopted to get information on their birth parents even still. Maybe yours will be one of those cases."

Nadia gave him a watery smile, her heart warming at his willingness to help her and provide her with the support she so desperately needed right now. "How can you be this nice? Like seriously, we just barely met."

Hector smiled back at her. "It's easy when I'm with you, to be honest. The thought of putting a smile on your face, of making you feel even just a little better, makes it all worth it."

Her heart beat a little faster at his words,

warming even more. "Well, I definitely would love to see where your idea might lead."

Hector reached out and brushed a stray hair off her forehead, leaving a tingle in her skin where his hand had brushed her. Nadia cast her eyes down, hoping he hadn't noticed her reaction and took a sip of coffee to buy herself a moment. Hector let go of her hand and did the same. Nadia took another sip and too much coffee sloshed up, almost choking her.

She spluttered a little, reaching for a napkin to wipe at some of the coffee that had dripped on the table and feeling supremely embarrassed. But, to her relief, Hector didn't laugh at her, he just offered her another napkin so that she could dab at the coffee on her chin.

"And you really think this might work?" she asked, turning the topic back to finding her birth mother.

Hector gave her a crooked smile. "There's only one way to find out."

CHAPTER FIVE

Nina rapped on Charlotte's back door and then let herself inside her sister's kitchen, shrugging off the jacket she'd worn against the early March breeze. Charlotte stood at the kitchen sink, rinsing some berries in a colander when Nina walked inside, slinging her jacket across the back of a kitchen table chair.

"Hey, sis, glad you could make it," Charlotte said, running her fingers through the berries to make sure they'd all gotten rinsed before setting the colander of berries aside to dry. "You're just in time to help me put the charcuterie board together."

"Oh, goodie, I'm starving," Nina replied, coming over to give Charlotte a quick hug.

"It's not for right now," Charlotte said, rolling her

eyes even as she smiled. "It's for when Mom gets here."

"I can't even sample it a little bit?"

Charlotte shook her head. "No, it needs to look perfect or else Mom will notice."

"Too true," Nina murmured. "Well, at least tell me you have something I can munch on while we wait. Pretty please?"

"Just because you said 'please'...I'm pretty sure I have some protein bars in the cupboard by the fridge."

Nina pulled a face, but walked over to the cupboard to help herself, rummaging through it until she found a flavor to her liking. She unwrapped the birthday cake flavored protein bar and bit into it, grimacing at the chalky texture and forcing herself to chew it and swallow it. Grudgingly, she took another bite, if only to appease the growling of her stomach. The second bite went down with even more difficulty than the first, so when Charlotte wasn't looking, she tossed the rest of the bar into the trash can, hiding it under an old napkin.

"I saw that," Charlotte said with a chuckle, and Nina jumped guiltily.

"Sorry! It's just... so gross."

Charlotte laughed aloud at that. "I know, that's

why I never eat them. Briggs uses them after he goes for a long run."

"How can he even eat them?"

"He says they taste good," Charlotte replied with a shrug.

Nina gaped at her, dumbfounded. "And you're sure you want to marry this guy?" she teased.

Charlotte pretended to think, then nodded. "Yeah, pretty sure. Come on, help me put this board together."

Together, the two sisters began arranging the fresh berries, dried apricots, artisan crackers, and wedges of brie cheese on a large wooden board, talking as they worked. Nina couldn't help but notice how carefully Charlotte was arranging everything, moving things over and over until they looked absolutely perfect. She could see that Melissa's impending visit was weighing on Charlotte. As if reading her mind, Charlotte spoke.

"I never had a chance to thank you for hosting Mom while she's in town," she said.

"Hey, it's the least I can do, especially since you have your wedding planning to focus on. Which, that's only two months away now! How are you feeling?"

"Good! We're keeping things simple, which is

helping out a ton in the planning department. How are things going with you and Oliver? I haven't hung out with both of you in a while."

Nina smiled, her cheeks warming. "I've never been this happy," she admitted. "And really, it's all thanks to you."

"Me?" Charlotte blinked. "How so?"

"Well, if you'd never moved to Sea Breeze Cove in the first place, I never would've had a reason to come visit you here. And if I'd never visited, I never would've fallen in love with the town... and a certain handsome doctor."

Charlotte reached out and hugged her sister. "I'm so glad you live close by. I never would've thought when I moved here and ended up running The Book Nook that I'd be lucky enough to have my younger sister move here too. And I'm glad things are going well for you and Oliver. Do you see a future there?"

Nina supposed her sister was asking this question because, in the past, Nina had been something of a serial dater, her relationships never lasting very long. She nodded.

"I do. In fact... I could see myself walking down the aisle to him at some point in the future, if you know what I mean."

Charlotte squealed, hugging Nina again. "Oh, I'm so happy for you!"

Nina laughed. "It hasn't happened yet, I'm just saying I'm open to it."

"I know, but that's a big deal for you!"

Nina smiled, returning to arranging some artisan crackers on the board. Just then, there was a firm knock at the front door. Before either of the sisters could go to answer it, Nina heard the front door open and Melissa's voice rang out through the house commandingly.

"Charlotte? Where are you, dear?"

"We're in the kitchen, Mom," Charlotte called back, hurrying to arrange the last of the apricots on the charcuterie board and then stepping back.

Melissa hurried down the hallway and entered the kitchen like a whirlwind. Suddenly, the large space felt a lot smaller, overcrowded even. Melissa hurried over to Nina and Charlotte, giving each of them a hug and kiss in turn, her signature perfume lingering in the air.

"Congratulations on your upcoming nuptials," Melissa said to Charlotte, leaning forward eagerly. "Now, you've bought the dress already, haven't you? I hope so, because you'll need time to make sure any alterations are finished correctly. Oh, and where is the venue? I'd like to see it and make sure there are no problems. A bad venue can just ruin things, you know. Oh, and the flowers—"

But here Charlotte raised her hand and stemmed the flow of her mother's words, chuckling a little. "Whoa, slow down, Mom. Take a deep breath, you've only just arrived."

Melissa looked mildly affronted. "Charlotte," she said imperiously, "I am here partially to make sure that your wedding planning is going well."

"That's very kind of you," Charlotte responded. "But things are well in hand."

"Are they? I notice that you didn't answer any of my questions."

Nina watched as Charlotte took a deep breath. "Briggs and I are having a joint wedding with some friends of ours, Elise and Gabe. We're planning to get married outside on the beach and then we're having our reception in a local bar. My dress is going to be simple, and I'll be sure to get it with enough time for alterations to be made."

Melissa pursed her lips, looking vaguely disappointed that Charlotte had things so well in hand. Pride surged through Nina at the way her sister had stood her ground with poise and respect. It filled her with awe. Melissa, seeming to realize she would get no further badgering Charlotte about her wedding, now turned to the charcuterie board, eyeing it carefully, but she didn't comment on it, which Nina knew meant that it had passed muster.

"Would you like to munch on this in the living room?" Nina asked, picking up the charcuterie board.

"Great idea," Charlotte said. "I'll grab some napkins."

A moment later, they were settled on the sofa and armchairs in the living room, the charcuterie board set out on the coffee table. Melissa reached over and picked up a cracker and placed some brie on it, popping it into her mouth and chewing. Again, she didn't say anything about it, which meant it met with her approval.

"Now, Nina, let's talk about you," Melissa said when she had swallowed her mouthful. "How are things going in your new relationship with the doctor?"

Nina quickly put a dried apricot into her mouth to buy herself some time before she had to answer. She chewed carefully and then finally swallowed. "I'm very happy."

Melissa raised an eyebrow. "Is that all I'm going to get? Tell me about this young man."

Nina smiled in spite of herself as she thought about Oliver. "He's amazing, Mom, I promise. He's a doctor, as you know, and he works so hard to ensure that the people of this town are well cared for when they come in to see him."

"I already knew all of that."

"Well, let's see... he likes walking on the beach and he loves swimming to keep up his fitness. He's a great cook too."

Melissa nodded in approval. "A man ought to know how to cook. He shouldn't expect the woman to do all of the cooking. That's 1950's thinking, and I don't approve of it."

"Oliver isn't like that. He treats me like a princess."

"As he should," Melissa said with authority, reaching for a blackberry on the board and popping it into her mouth. "I look forward to meeting your beau."

"Beau?" Charlotte said with a laugh. "Mom, no one uses that word anymore."

"Well, they should. It's a proper word and I detest a poor vocabulary."

Nina smiled at their banter, even as her stomach constricted a little. She nibbled on a cracker, hoping the salt would ease the nausea that threatened to ensue. Oliver had said that a pack of wild dogs couldn't tear him from her side, that he could certainly handle meeting her mother. But, she reflected, he had said that before meeting Melissa. Would he actually be able to handle the force of nature that was Melissa?

CHAPTER SIX

Shafts of late afternoon sunshine slanted into the room where Sadie was working. Even though she hadn't checked the time, she could tell by the angle of the sunlight entering the window that it was late afternoon and that the early evening sunset wasn't too far away. She paused in her work, setting her roller paint brush back into the tray of paint and stretching out her lower back, which was beginning to ache from all the painting. Groaning a little as she stretched out her lower back, she reminded herself to throw more yoga into her workouts so that she could ease up the cramped muscles from the repetitive work.

Silver napped in a shaft of sunlight near her. She had finally managed to train the exuberant dog not to step in the tray of paint while she was working, which made her job much easier. She looked around, surveying her work. This room, which would serve as Sadie and Addison's office, was nearly finished with painting, and it was looking stellar, in her humble opinion. Humming now, she picked up her roller brush again and was just about to begin painting when she heard the front door open.

"Yoohoo!" a voice called from the front room. "It's Addison!"

"I'm back in the office," Sadie called, sticking her head out into the hallway and waving to Addison, who was holding a brown bag.

Silver lifted his head from his paws as Addison walked into the room, blinking sleepily and giving a soft *woof* by way of greeting to the newcomer. Addison grinned, squatting down to scratch between his ears the way he liked it, then she stood and surveyed the room.

"You've made good progress!" she said, looking around and studying the newly painted room.

"Yup, I'll definitely get this room finished today, and then there are only a couple more rooms that need paint!"

"That's so awesome! I love seeing how much you and Ethan have done. Oh, I almost forgot," Addison said, lifting up the brown bag. "I brought you a snack. Figured you probably hadn't taken a break for lunch."

Sadie smiled appreciatively. "How did you know?"

Addison gave her a look. "I know you well enough by now to know that you forget to eat once you start working."

Sadie rubbed her hands together. "So, what did you bring me?"

"Open the bag and see."

Sadie set down her roller brush and took the brown paper bag from Addison, pulling it open. She pulled out a flatbread with a side of hummus infused with lemon juice and garlic. "Ugh, this looks amazing. Exactly what I needed."

Tearing the flatbread into smaller pieces, she dipped it into the hummus and popped it into her mouth, letting out a groan of pleasure as the flavors of the hummus melted on her tongue.

"Here, I brought you some coffee too," Addison said, handing over a to-go mug that Sadie hadn't noticed at first.

Sadie reached for it, taking a grateful sip and wincing as she burned her tongue a little bit in her haste. She set the coffee aside to cool down and dipped another piece of the flatbread into the hummus. Silver whined at her feet, looking up at her with pleading puppy dog eyes, which made her laugh.

"Oh, all right," she said, tearing off a plain bit of flatbread and tossing it to him. He jumped for it, catching it in the air and gobbling it down before sitting at her feet again, begging for more scraps. Sadie shook her head at him. "No more, sweetie. You only get the one piece."

Silver whined and huffed a little, but he settled back into his patch of sunlight, setting his head on his paws and looking like he was preparing to nap once more.

"So, I've been on the phone with several vendors," Addison said, tucking her hands into her jacket pockets.

"Oh, yeah?" Sadie said around a mouthful of flatbread and hummus. "How is that going?"

"Better than expected! I still have a few more to call, but I've been able to source some kennels for the kennel room and some of the parts we'll need for the dog washing station."

"That's awesome!"

"Oh, and a wholesale dog food vendor is supposed to get back to me soon. Fingers crossed that he comes through—his prices are better than anyone else's."

"You're so on the ball."

"So are you," Addison replied, smiling warmly. "You've been working your butt off in this house, making it look all fresh and new and it's amazing."

"Thanks! You know, I'd say we have the makings of a perfect team."

Addison gave Sadie a quick hug, her smile growing. "I was just thinking the same thing!"

"Speaking of perfect teams, I wonder how Charlotte and Elise are doing on the plans for their double wedding. I've been so busy over here that I haven't had a chance to check in with them for a while."

"Me neither," Addison admitted. "It's so exciting, but I'm worried about whether they'll be able to get everything done in time. I mean, planning a wedding is a huge undertaking."

"I know," Sadie said, swallowing a mouthful of flatbread smeared with hummus. "It also makes me wonder how quickly we can throw a double bridal shower together."

"If anyone can get it done in time, we can," Addison said bracingly. "We've got this!"

"I like your enthusiasm," Sadie said with a

chuckle. "At least Charlotte and Elise have two friends who are willing to move mountains to help them with the planning and execution of their wedding."

"Agreed. I'm willing to do whatever they need to get things done on time."

"Me too. We should check in with them soon and ask what we can do to help, even if it means putting our plans here on hold for just a little." Sadie took a sip of her now-cooler coffee and sighed with pleasure. "What do you think?"

"Sounds like a plan," Addison agreed. "This is a big day for them, and I want them to know we've got their backs."

"Great minds think alike. Now, how would you like to help me paint for a little bit?"

* * *

"There are so many dresses," Elise Sharpe said to Daisy, looking through the window of Beatrix's Bridal Shoppe. "We could be here all day!"

She suddenly felt overwhelmed.

Seeming to sense Elise's trepidation, the older woman took her arm and smiled at her. "Courage, dear. Remember, you only have to try on dresses that *you* like and only the ones in your size. See? It won't take all day."

"You're right," Elise agreed with a laugh. "I'm so glad you're with me today."

"I wouldn't have missed it for the world."

Arm in arm, the two women entered the shop and were greeted by Beatrix herself.

"Hello, ladies, what can I do for you today?"

Daisy piped up. "Elise here is getting married in a couple of months, and we want to find her the perfect dress."

"Congratulations!" Beatrix said to Elise. "You came to the right place, also. I'm confident that you'll find a dress you love today. So, what kind of styles were you thinking?"

"Um..." Elise gulped. She had no idea what would look good on her. "Maybe a mermaid style? Or a princess ball gown style? Or a simple sheath?"

Beatrix's eyes widened. "Those are all very different."

Elise blew out a breath. "I know... I guess I'm just overwhelmed and I'm not sure where to start."

Beatrix nodded knowingly and gave her a reassuring smile. "No need to worry, that's completely fine! Why don't I just start showing you dresses and you can tell me which ones catch your eye?"

Elise nodded gratefully. "That sounds perfect. Let's do it!"

Over the next twenty or so minutes, Beatrix led Elise and Daisy through the shop, showing them dress after dress and setting aside every one that Elise seemed partial to. They had all sorts of styles—from heavily beaded to light and ethereal unadorned silk—and Elise couldn't believe there were still more to see. Finally, she suggested it was time to try on the ones she had selected. Beatrix went into the fitting room to help her while Daisy waited on a cream plush sofa outside, sipping on a flute of champagne.

The first dress was a beaded mermaid style dress with a sweetheart neckline. Elise hated it the moment it was on her skin. The fabric pulled at her curves, highlighting every point on her body that she was self-conscious about. When she went out to show Daisy, Daisy was kind but shook her head to indicate that it was not the dress.

The next dress was a spaghetti strap silk dress with a slit up to the thigh. It looked elegant and simple on the hanger but when she put it on, Elise just wasn't sure. It looked a little *too* simple, like she was getting ready for an elegant event but not a wedding. Outside, Daisy looked her up and down appraisingly.

"It's beautiful..." she said, hesitating.

"But it's not right for my wedding," Elise finished for her.

"My thoughts exactly."

"Not to worry," Beatrix chimed in. "On to the next dress!"

But an hour, and many dresses later, Elise felt defeated and ready to cry. Despite the mountains of fabric she had waded through and tried on, she still had not found a dress that felt like it was made for her, nothing that just felt *right*. Beatrix was looking disappointed too, but she halfheartedly suggested they could go back to the racks and keep looking.

"No, I think I'm finished for today," Elise said, holding back tears. "Besides, Daisy and I were going to head to lunch."

"Well, you know where to find me when you're ready to keep looking," Beatrix said, smiling at them both.

Elise and Daisy thanked her, then headed out of the shop and down the street toward a new lunch cafe, Wright Wraps. Daisy tucked her arm through Elise's as they walked, not filling the silence between them, as though Daisy knew that Elise just needed time to think. In the restaurant, they sat by a window and ordered vegetable wraps bathed in a light olive oil along with some truffle fries sprinkled with parsley to go on the side. Soon, the two women were munching on their light lunch. Elise took a second bite of her wrap, barely tasting the subtle flavors. Finally, she pushed her plate aside, meeting Daisy's gaze for the first time since they'd left the shop.

"What if I can't find a dress?" she wailed quietly, tears stinging at her eyes. "That went horribly!"

Daisy reached out and took hold of her hands, smiling gently. "Take a deep breath, dear."

Elise complied and Daisy patted her hands.

"That's better," she said soothingly. "Now, here's what you need to remember, dear—Gabe is still going to want to marry you no matter what you wear. You could walk down the aisle in blue jeans and a t-shirt and he would still think you're the most beautiful woman he's ever seen."

Elise snorted, unable to help herself, and gave Daisy a watery smile. "I just might have to resort to that if the wedding dress shopping keeps going this badly."

"Well, let's not give up hope yet."

"I don't know if I can face going to another shop and striking out all over again."

Daisy patted Elise's hand again. "Well, let's not think about that yet. Right now all you have to focus on is finishing that delicious lunch of yours and taking deep breaths. It's all going to work out," she said serenely.

Elise complied, taking a bite of a truffle French fry and finding, to her surprise, that she was actually enjoying it.

"Wedding planning is notoriously stressful," Daisy continued, taking a sip of her lemon water. "But it's important to remember to enjoy the journey as much as you can. No matter what happens, the wedding will be wonderful because you're marrying the man you love most in this world."

Elise nodded, gratitude and peace settling over her. "That's so true," she murmured, reaching out to squeeze Daisy's hand. She was so thankful to have this good woman in her life. "Thank you for reminding me of what matters most."

"Anytime, dear. Anytime."

CHAPTER SEVEN

It took Sadie a moment to realize someone was talking to her as she painted, since she had her headphones in and was jamming out to ABBA while she worked. She wiggled and danced as she painted, singing along to "Waterloo" as she rolled the gray paint over the walls of the last unfinished room on the main floor.

"Sadie!"

Sadie jumped, pulling out one of her headphones and splattering paint onto the drop cloth that covered the floor as she whirled around. Jesse stood in the doorway, eyebrows raised and grinning at her.

"Were you calling me?"

"For like two minutes, yeah."

"Sorry," she responded, feeling sheepish, "I had my music turned up pretty loud."

"I can tell," Jesse teased, mimicking her dance moves and making her laugh aloud. "I was just letting you know that I finished putting up the new drywall in the bathroom and it should be ready for painting whenever you're ready."

"You already finished mudding the drywall and sanding it down?" Sadie was stunned at how quickly Jesse could work.

"Yes, ma'am, it's all finished and ready for you."

"Wow, you're amazing! Thank you so much— you saved us a lot of money not having to bring in a contractor to put up that drywall."

"Glad to be of service," Jesse said, giving her a mock salute. "Do you need anything else before I head out?"

Sadie thought about it, then shook her head. "No, I think I'm good. Say hi to Addison for me."

"Will do!" Jesse gave her a wave and then turned to leave.

Sadie turned back to her paint roller, dipping it into the tray of paint and continuing to paint the wall. She had meant what she said—they really *were* lucky that Jesse had been able to replace the drywall in the bathroom instead of having to hire a contractor to do it. When Sadie had gone in to paint the bathroom a few days before, she had discovered that some of the drywall was rotting with mold. Jesse had come in to take a look at it and had declared that the drywall needed to be replaced, something that had filled Sadie with stress. To her relief, though, Jesse had been able to complete the repair with minimal costs.

Sadie was just about to turn her music up again when she heard the front door open and then bounding footsteps coming down the hallway. She turned around to see Ethan hurrying into the room, his cheeks flushed and his sandy brown hair windswept. A general aura of excitement surrounded him, his moss-green eyes bright and wide with wonder.

"Sadie!" he called, rushing over to her. "I have huge news for you!"

"Whoa, whoa, slow down." Sadie laughed. "You're talking a mile a minute."

Ethan shook his head and bowled straight past that. "Sadie, this is seriously big news!"

Curiosity and excitement flooded through Sadie and she set her paint roller down, nerves and wonder buzzing through her now as well. Did Ethan's flurried state have something to do with the surprise he had been talking about a while before?

"What is it? Tell me, tell me!"

Ethan sucked in a deep breath, running a hand through his already tousled hair. "Okay, here it is—I got an email from a specialist in Boston and... he thinks that he might be able to fix my hand."

Sadie felt her jaw drop. "Are you serious?"

Ethan nodded enthusiastically. "I reached out a while ago—he's supposed to be the best around—but I didn't want to tell you in case things didn't pan out. But he just got back to me and he says he has high hopes that he can fix my hand!"

Sadie reached out and wrapped her arms around her boyfriend, holding him close. "E, that's such good news! I can't believe it!" she said, overwhelmed by the enormity of the news. "I know you've felt like you weren't completely 'whole' without your hand."

Ethan nodded against her hair. "But now there's a chance that I will be whole again."

"When do you meet with him?" Sadie asked, pulling back to look up into his face.

"I'll need to take some time away from Sea Breeze Cove soon," he replied, his eyes sparkling. "I'll meet with the doctor to consult with him and possibly get the surgery if all goes well."

"Should I come with you?"

Ethan smiled down at her, his expression soft. "No, but thank you, love."

"Are you sure?"

He nodded. "As much as I would love to have you there, you need to stay here and keep focusing on the kennel. I don't want this to distract you from your new business. I know it's like your baby."

"Well, yes," Sadie admitted. "But you're more important."

"I know, but that's why I can confidently say you should stay. I have no doubt that you'd love to be with me and that you would come if I asked you to. But I'm not. You should stay here and focus on getting the kennel ready."

"If you're sure..."

"I am," he said firmly, pulling her close again.

Sadie melted into his embrace, resting her head on his chest. She was grateful that Ethan wanted her to stay and keep working on the never-ending list of tasks she had to get the kennel ready, but she was also hit by a new worry, one that she would never voice aloud.

If Ethan's surgery was a success, would he still want to work with her on her business? Or would he return to his former work as a veterinarian?

If he did want to do that, she couldn't fault him. It had, after all, been his life's work before the accident that had turned his world upside down. Still, she had to admit to herself that losing him by her side for work every day would be a sad blow, and that he would be sorely missed by her.

Keeping her sad thoughts to herself, Sadie snuggled closer, hugging him more tightly around his waist. She didn't want her feelings inside to detract from this huge moment for him, especially because she truly *was* overjoyed for him. Pushing aside her worries, she tilted her head back and pressed a kiss to his lips.

Liz stepped out of the shower, reaching for a towel. She had just completed a grueling workout in the hotel gym and had been in sore need of a hot shower to soothe her aching muscles. Outside the hotel room windows, the sky was darkening as evening overcame Sea Breeze Cove. She toweled off, wrapping her dark hair in a second towel and padding into the bedroom area of her suite to pull on some flowy pajamas, even though it wasn't bedtime yet. All she wanted to do now was relax.

Back in the bathroom, she began working on her nighttime skincare routine, smoothing on some retinol serum. Liz was back in Sea Breeze Cove, having just returned from a trip to New York City for some work events that needed to be handled in person.

By now, she was basically splitting her time half and half between the small beach town and the big city. Thanks to remote work setups that were becoming more and more popular, she was able to manage her time this way, for which she was grateful.

Sure, some of the people back in New York were surprised that she wanted to spend so much time in the little town of Sea Breeze Cove, but what they didn't understand was how much this town had grown on her. It truly had worked its way into her heart, and she loved it more and more.

Of course, even more than that, she knew that the real reason she was choosing to spend so much time in this little town was her biological daughter, Nadia Bailey. Despite knowing who her daughter was and that she went to school in town, Liz still hadn't managed to decide what she should do in regard to Nadia. Should she introduce herself, try to build a relationship? She didn't know, and the question dogged at her night and day.

She had just finished smoothing on her moisturizer when she heard a knock at her hotel room door. .

Padding over to the door, Liz peered through the peephole and saw Andy Kaplan standing in the hallway, holding two takeout bags. Liz pulled open the door, a little embarrassed to be caught in her pajamas. At least, she reflected, she was wearing her most stylish matching set.

"Hey!" Andy said when she pulled open the door. He lifted up the takeout bags and gave her a friendly, hopeful smile. "I brought some food, and I was wondering if you'd like some company for dinner. Have you already eaten?" He caught sight of her pajamas and his brow puckered in confusion since it was only five p.m. "Or were you about to go to bed?"

Liz looked down at her pajamas and laughed. "No, I just wanted to be comfortable."

"I totally get that. Anyway, dinner? They're spinach salads with feta and grilled eggplant—super delicious."

Liz hesitated, not sure if she was up for company at the moment.

Seeming to read her mind, Andy turned away. "Sorry, I shouldn't have intruded."

Liz hurried to reach out and put a hand on his arm, stopping him from leaving. "No, no, you're not intruding at all. I would love some company, and dinner sounds delicious. Why don't you come in?"

Andy hesitated. "Are you sure?"

"Yes," Liz said firmly, opening the door wide for him.

Andy followed her into the suite, setting the takeout bags on the small bistro-style circular dining table and unpacking the salads. Liz took the seat across from him, her stomach rumbling with hunger.

"Your timing is perfect," she said lightly. "I'm starving."

"Perfect. I just hope you like the salad."

"I'm sure I will."

Liz picked up her fork, taking a bite of the salad but in reality she was barely tasting it. Her thoughts, once more, had turned to her long lost daughter. She was silent as they ate, focusing on her food and not realizing that she wasn't doing her part to keep up the conversation. Andy spoke a few times, trying to draw her out, but Liz didn't notice. Finally, Andy reached out and touched her hand, making her blink and look up at him.

"Hey," he said softly, his eyes troubled, "I don't want to speak out of turn, but... is everything okay? You seem... troubled."

Liz's heart softened at the tender look in his eyes. "I am troubled," she admitted softly. She didn't know Andy well enough to confide something as monumental as giving up her daughter for adoption, but she was touched by how much he seemed to care. "There's this big decision I'm grappling with right now, and, even though I've thought through it a million times, I'm still not sure what to do about it."

"That's got to be frustrating," Andy said sympathetically.

Liz nodded, pursing her lips. "It is," she finally said. "And it plagues me, night and day. I just keep going back and forth and I hate feeling like my mind is in so much tumult and chaos."

"I wish there was something I could do to help, but I understand that this is a decision you need to make on your own." Andy paused, then his eyes lit up. "Actually, maybe there is something I can do! I can't make the decision for you, but maybe I can help with your mind being in so much tumult. As you know, I'm a personal trainer, and exercise is so helpful in clearing the mind and bringing peace. If you'd like, I can offer you a free training session sometime."

Liz was touched by his willingness to help. Plus, she had to admit, she kind of liked him, so she wouldn't mind spending more time in his company.

"I just might take you up on that sometime in the future," Liz said, reaching for her fork again. "For now, though, I just appreciate your company."

Andy smiled, his blue eyes bright with kindness, and Liz's heart thumped. "Well, the offer will always be there, just so you know."

CHAPTER EIGHT

Charlotte sat cross-legged on the sofa, flipping through her wedding binder for what felt like the thousandth time since she had begun wedding preparations a few months ago.

As she flipped through her binder, she went over the plans she'd made again, looking to see what had been taken care of already and what still needed to be attended to. Her mother, of course, had wanted to see the binder the first day she had come to visit, and she had been full of 'suggestions' that were more like commands when she rifled through its pages.

"You can't have your reception in a bar!" she had exclaimed, seeming scandalized that Charlotte would even consider such a thing. "It's simply not done! We'll find you a beautiful venue that will be much more suitable."

With Nina's help, Charlotte had managed to stand firm in the plans she had made with Elise, explaining that the local bar was where they wanted to celebrate with their friends and family, that they wanted to keep the atmosphere casual and fun, and that they wanted to keep decorations to a minimum.

Melissa had pursed her lips at that, seeming ready to argue about it, but Nina had jumped in, reminding their mother that it was Charlotte's wedding, and therefore *she* was the one who got to make the final decisions.

Briggs poked his head into the living room just then, pulling Charlotte from her thoughts. "Hey, babe, how's it going?" Catching sight of the binder in her lap, he came into the room and walked over to her. "Working on the wedding?"

"Trying to," she replied, running her fingers through her hair and sighing.

"Oh, I forgot to tell you, I spoke with Brady and he locked down the date of the reception for the bar. It's all ours."

"Thank you!" Charlotte exclaimed, crossing that off of the to-do list at the front of the binder. "I'm so glad that all worked out. I was worried he would say no."

"I think he's excited to be hosting a reception in his bar. It's good for business."

"Well, I'm glad we've gotten that reserved. How are things coming with the white chairs for the beach ceremony? Were you able to source any?"

Briggs nodded. "I'm still haggling with the vendor over the price, but I think we'll get those reserved any day now. He's on the verge of giving me a fair price, I can just feel it."

Charlotte laughed. "I'm glad you're taking care of the haggling and not me. That's just not my thing."

"I'm happy to do it," Briggs assured her, leaning down to kiss her on the forehead. "Anything you need me to do today?"

"Actually," Charlotte said, closing her binder and smiling up into his eyes, "you can't be a part of what I'm working on today."

"Oh?"

"Yup," Charlotte said blithely. "So, scram," she teased.

"Yes, ma'am," he said meekly, though his blue eyes twinkled. "I'll get out of your hair then."

Charlotte unfolded her legs and got up from the

sofa, wrapping her arms around his waist and kissing him softly. "Have a good day at work, love."

Briggs kissed her back. "With that send-off, I think it's bidding to be a great day."

Charlotte laughed and waved as Briggs headed for the front door. When he had left, the front door closing behind him, she hurried up to her room and pulled out the large box she had hidden in her closet.

She had gone online shopping the week before, ordering a handful of wedding dresses and they had arrived yesterday while Briggs had been at work. She had been careful to hide the box from him and, now that he had left for work today, she could begin the process of trying dresses on. She knew from Elise that her own search had not been going well, but Charlotte wasn't too worried about finding a dress.

She had no desire to find the 'perfect' dress for her ceremony, simply wanting something that looked flattering so that she could feel beautiful on her special day. The dress was really the least of her concerns, and she was certain that something in the box would work out.

Grabbing a pair of scissors from her desk, she sliced the tape on the box and pulled it open, lifting out the first dress. It was an A-line cut with spaghetti straps and lace details. Quickly stripping, she slid the lacy dress on and turned to look at herself in the mirror. The dress pulled in at her waist, accentuating her hourglass figure and then flowed out elegantly to pool slightly on the floor.

"Not bad," she mused, turning this way and that in the mirror.

She grabbed her phone and took a couple of mirror selfies, which she sent to her mom and sister. She hadn't wanted them to be there for her trying on the dresses, knowing that she wanted a quiet day, but she still cared about what they thought. Almost instantly, her phone buzzed as texts poured in.

NINA: OMG, I love it! So, so, so stunning!

MELISSA: Pretty, but is it too simple? I think you need more pizzazz.

Charlotte laughed aloud at her mother's judgmental text, but she wasn't hurt by it. She had known that Melissa wanted her to pick something extremely fancy and one-of-a-kind, but she had no interest in that. Taking one last look at her reflection in the mirror and deciding that she liked this dress and that it was definitely a contender, Charlotte pulled off the dress and set it carefully on her bed, then turned to pick up the next dress. This one was filmy and light, A-line again, with simple straps and almost no detailing.

She pulled the dress on and studied her reflection in the mirror. This one, though ethereal and light, had a few too many layers for picking up sand on the beach. Besides, it didn't accentuate her waist as beautifully as the first dress had.

Deciding the dress was just okay, Charlotte took it off and set it aside carefully. The next dress was a midi-length silk tube-top dress. She pulled it on, pleased with how light it was, but instantly began laughing as she looked in the mirror. She looked like a bride ready to be married in a courthouse, all business-like. She snapped a picture and sent it to her mother and sister. As before, the texts rolled in quickly.

MELISSA: No. Just no.

NINA: It's... something, that's for sure.

CHARLOTTE: It's definitely something. Not for me!

Charlotte was just about to try on the next dress, when she heard a knock at the front door. Her eyes flew open wide as she remembered that she was supposed to have a meeting with Liz about her book.

Hastily, she peeled off the dress and flung it onto the bed, hopping on one foot as she tried to pull her jeans on and almost falling over. She pulled her t-shirt on over her head, pausing only long enough to smooth her auburn hair down so she didn't look crazy and then raced down the stairs, pulling the front door open.

"Liz, hi!" she cried, stepping back so that the literary agent could step into the foyer. "Sorry to keep you waiting."

"Is this a bad time?"

"No, no," Charlotte assured her, shutting the door. "I just lost track of time, that's all. Want to sit in the living room? Can I get you a coffee? Some tea?"

Liz shook her head, smiling. "No, I'm fine. I just had brunch."

The two women settled on the sofa and Liz opened up her laptop, scrolling until she found her notes. "So, here's what I'm thinking about the latest revisions you made," she said, and they dove into the meeting.

For the next half hour, they discussed Charlotte's book, which was nearly finished, and talked about the changes Charlotte had made. Liz explained which publishers she had contacted about the book and mentioned that she'd received very positive responses from some of them, which sent Charlotte over the moon with excitement. She'd already had one lifelong dream come true when she'd become the owner of The Book Nook, and now she was close to achieving another dream that had once seemed impossible.

After that, they discussed the next steps in the publication process, and they agreed upon a date by which Charlotte could have the book finished.

"There's still plenty of work to do," Charlotte said as the meeting wrapped up, "but I'm confident that I can finish by the deadline."

"Good. And I'm confident that you'll have no trouble snagging a good publisher. It's a great book, and they're seeing that."

"Thank you," Charlotte said sincerely, leaning back against the sofa. "So, you're back in town again? Sea Breeze Cove must really be growing on you."

To her surprise, Liz's professional demeanor crumbled a bit and she looked away. "It's... yes. It's a very special place," Liz murmured, her voice thick with tears.

Alarm grew in Charlotte. Something was clearly wrong, but she wasn't sure if it was appropriate to ask Liz about what was going on. After all, Liz was her agent—should she really get personal? On the other hand, she had come to really like Liz, and she hated to see her in distress. Making her decision, Charlotte slipped out of business mode and allowed herself to treat Liz the way she would any of her friends.

"Liz?" she asked softly. "Is something wrong?"

Liz shook her head at first, but a moment later, she nodded. "I haven't told anyone this," Liz said, her voice choked, "but the real reason I keep coming back to this town is that my daughter lives here."

"I didn't know you had a daughter!"

Liz dabbed at her eyes. "No one does—I gave her up for adoption when she was born, and it was a closed adoption, so I never knew where she had gone. It wasn't until recently that I learned her name and where she lived."

Charlotte could feel that her eyes were wide as saucers, but she couldn't help it. The news was just too stunning. When she could speak, she asked, "Have you met her yet?"

Liz shook her head. "I haven't been able to bring myself to do it yet."

Charlotte's heart swelled with sympathy. "What's her name?" she asked quietly.

"Nadia Bailey."

Charlotte felt her jaw drop as she gasped. "Are you serious?"

Liz nodded.

"Oh my..." Charlotte pondered this. "Do you

know what you're going to do next?" she asked tentatively.

Liz looked at her with watery eyes, fresh tears gathering at the corners. "I'm so torn," she whispered. "Part of me wants to tell Nadia the truth as soon as possible, but... but what if she hates me?"

"Why would she hate you?" Charlotte cried.

"Because I gave her up," Liz said simply, her voice cracking as a tear trickled down her cheek.

Charlotte reached over and gently patted Liz's back, unsure of what to do. "Is there anything I can do to help you?"

Liz shook her head. "You have more than enough on your plate writing a book and planning a wedding."

"But connecting with your daughter is so important. I really do want to help."

Liz dabbed at her dark brown eyes, wiping away the salty tears that were making tracks down her cheeks. Charlotte's phone buzzed and she pulled it out, looking at it to give Liz some semblance of privacy for a moment. She saw a text from Addison.

ADDISON: Hey, girl! Just wanted to let you know that Sadie and I are planning a bridal shower for you and Elise! Obviously the soon-to-be husbands are invited too! Get ready to party!

CHARLOTTE: Aw, thanks! I can't wait!

Charlotte set her phone aside, an idea coming to her. Nadia would likely be at the bridal shower, seeing as how she was such good friends with Addison. She turned to Liz, her heart hammering in her chest at the audacity of what she was about to propose.

"Liz," she said, waiting until the older woman looked at her. "My friends are throwing me and Elise a bridal shower. Would you like to come?"

* * *

"It's no use!" Nadia cried, sitting back from the laptop and clenching her fists in frustration. "We're never going to find more information about my birth parents!"

Hector, who was sitting beside her, reached out and squeezed her hand. "Hey, don't say that. I know it's been slow going so far, but we shouldn't give up. I promise, I'm here and I'm ready to do whatever it takes to help you."

Nadia sighed. "I'm just not sure it's worth it anymore," she admitted. "I've been trying to rebuild my relationship with my adoptive parents individually, now that they're single people instead of a couple. That's a ton to deal with right there, and I don't know if it's a good idea to add even more to my plate, emotionally."

"Are you sure?"

Nadia shook her head. "No," she admitted, "I'm not. But maybe it's time to let sleeping dogs lie for a while." On a whim, she leaned over and pecked his cheek. "But thank you for how willing you've been to help me."

"Any time," Hector assured her, his cheeks a little flushed.

Nadia stood. "I have to run." Before she could pack away her laptop, a thought occurred to her. "Hey, I'm actually going to a bridal shower celebration thingy at Addison and Jesse's place in a few days—want to come? I mean, it'll be mostly ladies, but Jesse and the two grooms-to-be will be there."

"Are you sure it would be okay?"

Nadia nodded. "The more the merrier. I really would love for you to be my guest."

Hector grinned, nodding. "I'm sorry I couldn't be more help in your quest to find your birth parents, but I'll be honest that I'm really happy to have another reason to spend more time with you."

Nadia couldn't help but smile as her heart

turned over in her chest. "I feel the same way," she admitted, her voice a little shy.

And with that, before Hector could see how much she was blushing or how wide her smile had grown, Nadia waved and headed out of his office, hurrying toward campus for class.

CHAPTER NINE

Charlotte was still mulling over her decision to invite Liz to the bridal shower a full week after the fact. Should she really have forced a meeting between Nadia and Liz, even if her heart was in the right place and her intentions were pure? Maybe she was doing both of them a disservice. Charlotte had mulled over these thoughts again and again throughout the week.

Suddenly, a thought occurred to her—should she tell Addison? After all, Nadia was living with Addison at the moment and surely Addison of all people would know more about the situation. Charlotte was just reaching for her phone to shoot off a quick text to her friend when she paused, suddenly unsure of herself. Addison might already know that Nadia had been adopted, but she certainly didn't know who Nadia's birth mother was, and that wasn't really Charlotte's information to share. All she could hope for now was that Liz and Nadia would meet organically at the wedding shower tomorrow. She had meddled by inviting Liz—she certainly shouldn't meddle any further.

Decided, Charlotte pushed her phone back into her pocket, just as the back door opened and Briggs came into the kitchen, where she had been trying to decide what to make for dinner. At least, she had been before she got distracted by worries about having invited Liz to the wedding shower. Briggs held Bruno's leash still, having just taken the dog for his evening walk, and he now unclipped it so that Bruno could roam freely through the house, then walked over and kissed Charlotte lightly on the lips.

"Thanks for taking Bruno out," she said, taking the leash from him and hanging it on its hook by the back door.

"Not a problem. It was gorgeous out tonight—you should've come."

"I know," Charlotte agreed. "And I stayed back so I could start dinner and look at me—dinner isn't even begun yet."

"Having a hard time deciding what to make?"

Charlotte shook her head. "No, I just got lost in my own thoughts." She glanced at the clock. "We'll have to make something quick at this point, or we'll be eating well after dark."

"How about some chicken fettuccine alfredo?"

Charlotte grinned. "You really know the way to a girl's heart. When have I ever turned down a good Italian dish?"

"Pasta fills the soul," Briggs teased, already heading to the cabinet to pull out some fettuccine noodles.

"Amen," Charlotte said with a laugh. "I'll start cooking some chicken."

They worked together in companionable silence for a few minutes, the only sound the chicken frying in a pan and the water in the pot on the stove beginning to boil. Charlotte was just about to turn on some soft music when Briggs spoke.

"So... we've never discussed where we want to go on our honeymoon."

Charlotte blinked, surprised. "You're so right! How did we miss that in all of the wedding planning?"

"It's only the best part," Briggs teased. "I'd have thought it would be a priority."

"And so it should be," Charlotte said firmly.

"Any ideas? I haven't given it much thought yet, to be honest."

"Well, give it some thought," Briggs said lightly. "Come on, what sounds good to you?"

Charlotte closed her eyes, thinking. "Well, it's been so chilly lately, that somewhere warm and tropical sounds just about perfect."

"I couldn't agree more," Briggs agreed, leaning down to kiss Charlotte on the top of her head, then returned to stirring the fettuccine noodles, which were now at a roaring boil.

"Well, that was easy." Briggs laughed a moment later. "Are you sure there's nowhere else you've been dying to go? Maybe Paris? Or London?"

Charlotte shook her head. "Too crowded. Besides, I just want to relax on a beach somewhere, not go sightseeing."

"Once again, I totally agree with you," Briggs said with a laugh. "I thought maybe we could push ourselves to broaden our horizons, but that isn't really what a honeymoon is all about."

"I just want to spend time with you and bask in the sunshine," Charlotte said, rubbing her hands together in anticipation, her eyes alight with excitement. "I can already feel the sand between my toes!"

"And see the crystal clear blue water!" Briggs added, clearly excited as well. "Okay, I'm sold. A tropical beach resort it is."

"Yay!" Charlotte wrapped her arms around Briggs's waist and leaned up on her tiptoes for a kiss.

"I'll make all the arrangements," Briggs said when they broke apart. "You don't have to worry about a thing."

"Thank you," she replied fervently.

"You deserve the perfect honeymoon. And I'm going to make sure you get it, love."

Ethan looked around the sterile waiting room, anxiety clogging his throat. The walls were painted a minty green, the kind he had seen in far too many hospitals, and it filled him with dread. What if things didn't go as planned? What if the doctor told him there was actually nothing that could be done about his hand? While he knew, deep down, that Sadie would love him either way, he was still filled with the desire to be back at full strength so that he could be the man his love deserved the most. She had been so patient, so supportive, through this whole journey, and he didn't want to return to her, still a broken man.

Ethan took a few deep breaths, trying to quell the nausea that threatened to rise and to push away the anxiety. He closed his eyes, trying to remind himself over and over again that the specialist had been optimistic when they'd communicated in the past. He had nearly lowered his heart rate back to normal when the receptionist called his name. His eyes shot open and he stood, his heart once more hammering in his chest.

"Dr. Liang can see you now," the receptionist said, giving him a reassuring smile. "You can go on back."

"Thank you," Ethan replied, hoping his voice sounded steadier than he felt.

On leaden feet, he walked past the reception desk and down the hallway until he came to the door with the nameplate that read 'Dr. Jen Liang'. Taking in one more steadying breath, Ethan rapped lightly on the door, pushing it open when a voice inside told him to enter. Dr. Liang looked up from some paperwork she had been working on, tucking her glossy dark hair behind her ear and rising to greet him, one hand stretching out to shake his. They shook hands and then she gestured to a chair across from hers for him to sit. Ethan sat heavily, his heart still pounding so hard he was surprised she couldn't hear it.

"Ethan, it's so nice to finally meet you in person," Dr. Liang said. "Thank you for coming out to meet me. I know it's a bit of a trip for you."

"Thank you for seeing me," he replied, pleased that his voice was becoming steadier.

"May I see your hand?"

Ethan nodded, stretching out his injured hand. Dr. Liang leaned over it, turning it this way and that as she examined it.

"I was fairly certain from the photos you sent that I could help you," she began, and Ethan suddenly felt foreboding. Was she going to say that things had changed now? "However, now I'm confident that I can fix your hand."

Ethan let out his breath in a rush, exultation and excitement flooding through him. "Really?"

Dr. Liang nodded, her eyes twinkling. "Really."

Ethan stared down at his injured hand, picturing it whole and well, with full range of motion and dexterity. The thought overwhelmed him with joy and excitement for the future. He would be getting his life back!

"I have more good news for you," she continued.

Ethan looked up. "Really? What's that?"

Dr. Liang folded her hands on her desk and leaned forward. "One of my surgeries today was canceled at the last minute, so I can fit you in for surgery. Today."

Ethan blinked, staring at her uncomprehendingly. He wasn't sure he had heard her correctly. "Today?"

"Today," she confirmed.

A part of Ethan hesitated. It was all so soon. He wanted his hand fixed, but he had wanted Sadie by his side when he woke up from his operation.

Seeing his hesitation, Dr. Liang spoke again. "I know it's sudden, but it's a real opportunity for you. I'm a very busy surgeon, and my schedule is booked out for months. This opening is a good chance for you to get your hand fixed quickly. If you opt out of the surgery today, I can't guarantee you a spot in the near future."

Ethan nodded, taking in the enormity of the situation. As much as he wanted Sadie with him, he knew that he wouldn't get another chance like this. Swallowing, he made his decision and nodded at Dr. Liang.

"Thank you for offering me the spot," he said, his throat dry. "I'll take it!"

"Very good," Dr. Liang said approvingly and rose from her desk. "I'll speak to my nurse to get you prepped for surgery."

Ethan stood as well, shaking hands with her once more before she hurried out of the room to find her nurse. Ethan fished his phone from his pocket. He couldn't get Sadie here in time, but he would text and let her know the joyous news. He tapped on her contact and paused for a moment, his thumbs hovering over the keypad.

ETHAN: Sadie? You're never going to believe this... but the doc said she can schedule my surgery for today. Next time I see you, my hand will be fixed.

CHAPTER TEN

Ethan had been on Sadie's mind all day. She had awoken wondering how he was doing and the thoughts of him and his visit to the specialist were never far from her thoughts as she got up and went about her daily routines. She wanted to reach out and ask how he was doing, but she didn't want to bother him, especially on such an important day. By early afternoon, though, she was dying for some more information and it was getting harder and harder to be patient.

She was out walking dogs for clients and had taken on an extra-large load to help her pass the time —four dogs, two leashes in each hand. The April sunshine overhead warmed her, though it didn't actually bring much heat. She knew all the heat was coming from her speed walk and trying to contain four exuberant dogs on their leashes. She was just coming to the top of a hill that ended in a gorgeous view of Sea Breeze Cove's beach when she felt her phone buzz in her pocket. Was it Ethan? She was dying to check, but she couldn't, not with four leashes in her hands. She would just have to wait until later to check, even though the waiting was excruciating.

After what felt like hours but was only another half hour or so, Sadie had returned all the dogs to their homes and was heading with Silver to the new property that would become their doggy boarding house. She parked the car in front of the property and let herself into the house, finally pulling her phone from her pocket and seeing that Ethan had indeed messaged her. She tapped on the message and read it quickly.

ETHAN: Sadie? You're never going to believe this... but the doc said she can schedule my surgery for today. Next time I see you, my hand will be fixed.

Sadie gaped down at her phone, not believing her eyes. She slid down the wall in the main room until she sat on the floor, her knees up to her chest as she read the message over and over. Conflicting emotions warred within her—elation for Ethan and this opportunity mingled with worry for him and the wish that she could be there with him. She knew some time had passed since he had sent the message, but maybe he hadn't gone into surgery yet. She quickly tapped out a reply.

SADIE: That's amazing news, my love! Wish I could be with you! <3 <3 <3

The message was wholly inadequate to express everything she was feeling, but she figured that would have to do until she saw him again in person. After all this time, it was crazy to think that Ethan would be returning to her with a fixed hand, if everything went according to plan. And oh, for his sake, how she hoped it would. She set her phone aside, pulling her knees closer to her chest and scratching Silver between his ears as worries for Ethan began to engulf her. What if something went wrong and his hand couldn't be fixed? Would he ever be able to recover emotionally from that? It had been hard enough the first time.

She was just about to give way to her fears completely when the front door opened and Addison stepped inside.

"I thought I'd find you here! Ready to discuss the bridal shower?" Addison said cheerfully, then paused, taking in the scene of

Sadie sitting on the floor snuggled up with Silver. She faltered, her smile disappearing and her brow furrowing with worry. "Is something wrong?"

Sadie nodded and then shook her head. "Yes? No? Maybe?"

Addison came over to sit cross-legged in front of her. "That doesn't really answer my question, you know."

Sadie sighed, rubbing at her forehead which had begun to ache dully. "Ethan is in Boston seeing a specialist about his hand."

"That's good news, isn't it?"

Sadie nodded. "Apparently, the doctor said she could schedule his surgery for today."

Addison gasped and clapped her hands. "That's wonderful! Usually surgeries like that are booked out for months!"

"It is wonderful," Sadie said, but tears were beginning to fill the corners of her eyes.

"Oh, Sadie..." Addison leaned forward and rested her hand on Sadie's arm. "What's really going on? I know you're happy for Ethan, but there's something else going on too, isn't there?"

Sadie nodded. "It's just... aside from my worries about whether or not the surgery will go well, I'm worried about what our lives are going to look like when he gets back."

"What do you mean?"

Sadie gulped in a deep breath, willing herself not to cry. "Well, if his hand is fixed, what if he doesn't want to work on our business together anymore? We became partners, but now maybe he'll want to go back to being a vet. Which," she hastened to add, "is fine! Being a veterinarian was his whole life, but I got used to having him as my business partner and now I can't imagine doing all this without him!"

Addison nodded sympathetically, taking in Sadie's words. Finally, she spoke. "I know this isn't exactly the same, but when Jesse and I were going through his health trial, I had so many fears and worries about the future. I was afraid nothing would ever be the same again between us."

"I know that was a really scary time for you," Sadie murmured.

Addison nodded. "But we got through it together and, trust me, having Ethan at full strength is only going to enhance your relationship, no matter what path he chooses career-wise."

Sadie sniffed, nodding now too. "You're so right. I was getting so lost in my worries about what this will mean for my business that I forgot that this is something he's been wanting for such a long time. Who cares about the business? What matters most is that Ethan will be whole again and *feel* whole again."

"I mean, *I* care about the business, and so do you," Addison teased her gently.

"Well, right," Sadie amended with a blush. "That's not what I meant."

"I know, just joking. Feeling any better?"

Sadie nodded, leaning forward to hug her friend. "Thank you for reminding me of what's important."

"Any time, friend. You would do the same for me."

Sadie wiped at her eyes, leaning back against the wall and blowing out a deep breath. Addison looked around the empty room.

"So, when are we going to get some kennels installed in here?" Addison asked.

Sadie looked around the room too. "We still need to get them ordered, but I think I've found a vendor for the right price. They'll look really good too." She frowned. "Ethan might be too busy to install them if he's back at work as a vet, though."

"Not to worry on that front," Addison assured her. "My Jesse is strong, willing, and able to aid in that part of the setup process. You can take that worry off your plate."

"Good!" Sadie scrambled to her feet. "We still need to measure the room and take down the measurements of how many kennels we can fit in here. I brought a tape measure. Want to help me?"

"Sure thing." Addison clambered to her feet as well and so did Silver, barking happily and spinning in circles as he tried to be helpful, making both of the women laugh.

Sadie pulled her tape measure out of her jacket pocket and the two women began to measure the room, talking as they did so about the upcoming bridal shower and what they needed to do to get ready for it to be perfect for the two happy couples.

CHAPTER ELEVEN

Addison surveyed the balloon arch made of a myriad of silver, white, and cream balloons and pronounced it perfect, then bustled back over to the tables in Firefly Bistro where she still needed to arrange the flowers for the centerpieces.

"Mama, Mama, can I help?" Lainey asked, tugging at Addison's flowy maxi skirt and bouncing back and forth on the balls of her feet.

Addison gave her exuberant daughter a quick smile. "Of course, sweetie." She looked around, trying to find something that her daughter could do that wouldn't be very easily ruined, settling on a table in the back corner. "Come with me," she said, taking her daughter's hand and leading her over to the tucked-away table. "See this vase? I need you to put all the flowers in it really carefully. Make it look beautiful for mommy, okay?"

"I can do it!" Lainey exclaimed, her eyes glowing as she looked at the flowers with glee.

"I know you can," Addison responded, tousling Lainey's curls before returning to the front of the bistro.

She picked through her box containing clear plastic bags of candied hearts, setting a little bag at each seat for all of the tables, humming as she worked to soothe her nerves. People would be arriving soon and she still needed to arrange the flowered centerpieces for each of the tables. Time was simply moving too quickly and she had too much to do, but she forced herself to take a deep breath and reminded herself that it likely wouldn't take as long to finish preparations as she thought it would.

Fifteen minutes later, she stared around herself in surprise, pleased to see that she had indeed finished the centerpieces long before she thought she would. Relief flooded through her and she stretched out her back and neck, rolling her head from side to side and taking what felt like her first real breath that day. Spotting Sadie helping Lainey at the tucked-away table in the back, Addison headed over to them.

"Sadie," she called, pulling her friend aside. "Have you heard anything from Ethan yet?"

Sadie nodded, smiling at her friend. "He's out of surgery and in recovery. According to the doctor, he should be able to come home in the next day or two!"

"That's amazing! It sounds like the surgery went well."

"That's what the doctor said," Sadie replied cheerfully, her smile growing.

Addison threw her arms around her friend. "This is such good news! I'm so happy for both of you." She pulled back, looking into Sadie's eyes. "And remember what we talked about—Ethan returning to full strength will only help your relationship with him, not hurt it, even if he decides to go back to being a vet."

"I know," Sadie said softly. "I keep reminding myself of that."

"Good."

Just then, Bridget Clark bustled out of the bistro's kitchen and, seeing them, headed over to greet them.

"Hi, ladies!"

"Hey, Bridget," Addison and Sadie chorused, smiling at their friend.

"Hey, I've been meaning to ask you," Sadie said,

leaning forward a little. "How are things going with Timothy? I haven't talked to you in forever and I know you've got news. Dish, girl!"

Bridget laughed, her smile widening and her eyes sparkling with happiness. "I'm happier than I've ever been," she admitted. "I didn't know one person could be this happy."

"Awww, that's wonderful," Sadie replied, clapping her hands. "We're so happy for you!"

"Yes, we are," Addison added.

"Timothy is just... so wonderful," Bridget continued, looking dreamy. "He's so sweet to me and he always finds a way to make me smile. Did you know he came over this morning, super early, and made me pancakes so that I wouldn't have to make myself breakfast?"

"That's so sweet!" Addison exclaimed, beaming at her friend. "But tell me this—did the pancakes have bananas in them?"

Bridget grinned. "Even better—he put chocolate chips in them."

"Ugh, so good," Addison groaned, even as her stomach grumbled, making all three friends laugh. "I can't wait until we can eat," she added.

"Well, the food is going to be fantastic," Bridget promised. "It will be well worth the wait."

"Promise?" Addison teased.

"Promise!"

Just then, the bell at the front door jingled and the ladies turned around to see Nina walk through the door, followed closely by Melissa, who was close behind her.

Nina smiled at the sight of Addison, Bridget, and Sadie standing together and began walking over to them, her mother close on her heels. Her mother tugged on her arm, forcing her to stop. Nina turned, biting back upset words as Melissa surveyed the bistro with a critical eye.

"Look at these floral arrangements," Melissa said in a stage whisper, loud enough that Nina was sure the other women could hear it. "They're simply amateur! And carnations? Isn't that a bit trite? A bit cliche?"

"Mom," Nina breathed, feeling heat rush to her cheeks.

She forced herself not to look over at Addison and Sadie, whom she knew had both been working overtime for this wedding shower. Embarrassment flooded her stomach, and she felt a little sick. She wished for a moment that a sinkhole would open up in the floor right below her and that she could melt out of sight.

Melissa seemed not to hear her as she wandered over to the long table laid out with the foods for the shower—hummus and prosciutto wraps paired with similar sandwiches stuffed with baby greens and goat cheese. Melissa surveyed it all with her laser-like focus, her lips pursed with something that looked like disapproval.

"I had hoped for something fancier to celebrate your sister," she commented, folding her arms.

"Mom!" Nina whispered again, then closed her eyes and swallowed. It was time to be firm. "Charlotte and Elise are going to love it. All that really matters is that they're celebrating with all of their closest friends."

"Of course." Melissa nodded, but as she wandered away, Nina could still hear her murmuring criticisms under her breath.

Nina felt her face fall, and she lifted her hands to cover her eyes for a moment. A few seconds later, she felt a light touch on her shoulder and she moved her hands to see that Bridget had approached her, a sympathetic look on her face.

"Is everything okay?" Bridget asked softly,

searching Nina's eyes with her own. From the look on her face, it was clear that she could tell Nina was struggling.

Nina wrapped her arms around herself, biting her lip. "Um... would you believe me if I said yes?"

Bridget shook her head. "Not for a minute. What's going on?"

Nina sighed, shaking her head now too. "It's my mother. It's been... a little bit difficult having her in Sea Breeze Cove."

"Has she been staying with you?"

Nina nodded. "That's made it even more intense. She's with me all the time. There's no escape!"

Bridget laughed a little. "I'm sure that hasn't been easy."

"That's an understatement," Nina muttered. She rubbed at her forehead. "I don't mean to sound ungrateful. I mean, I love my mom and I'm glad she came to visit but..."

"But that doesn't mean it isn't wearing on you," Bridget finished for her, and Nina nodded gratefully.

"The worst part is, since my mom is staying at my apartment with me, I can't have Oliver over in the evenings."

"Does your mom hate him?"

Nina shook her head. "It's not that. It's more that I don't want to subject him, and our relationship, to my mother's constant scrutiny, you know? It's just easier not to have him over."

"Ah. I see."

"He used to come over most days and we would make dinner together, maybe watch a movie or take a walk or play games or something. Now I barely see him."

Bridget frowned sympathetically. "That must be so hard. I can't imagine being away from Timothy for that long." Her eyes brightened as an idea occurred to her. "You know, if it would help you, Timothy and I can step out for a bite to eat one night, leaving my apartment free. You and Oliver could use it to have some alone time."

Nina blinked, stunned at Bridget's words. "You would do that for me? Why?" she asked, before she could stop herself.

Bridget laughed. "Hey, I understand more than anyone the need to work through relationship troubles. It's definitely worth the work."

Nina laughed too. "I couldn't agree more." She laid a hand on Bridget's arm. "And, I might take you up on your offer. I'm becoming desperate."

"Just name the day. Nothing would make

Timothy or me happier than to help you and Oliver out."

"Thanks so much. I seriously appreciate it."

"Don't mention it!" Bridget looked over at the kitchen and saw Elise waving to her. "Oh, I'd better go."

"Okay, talk to you later," Nina said, snagging a wrap from the tray by her side as Bridget walked toward the swinging kitchen doors.

She bit into the prosciutto and hummus wrap, savoring the flavors and thinking to herself that, despite what her mother might say about the food, it was simply delicious. She chewed thoughtfully, her mood lighter than it had been in days as she thought about getting to spend an evening alone with Oliver soon.

Nina closed her eyes, picturing Oliver's handsome face, his hazel eyes that twinkled behind his glasses, his strong hand in hers. She had missed spending time with him, had missed his interesting conversation and the feel of his arms around herself. To think that she would soon get to enjoy that again, thanks to Bridget, lifted her mood more than words could say. And those happy thoughts propelled her to actually look forward to the wedding shower as she opened her eyes and looked around at the decorated room.

With the balloon arch and the floral centerpieces, everything looked stunning, and she hoped that Charlotte and Elise, as well as their fiancés, would love it.

As she finished up her wrap and saw Bridget coming out of the kitchen with a tray of clean glasses to set on the table, Nina smiled at her. She hadn't been sure if Bridget liked her for a while, especially when she herself had tried to date Timothy Parsons, but now she knew that she and Bridget were friends.

And with her critical mother in town, it was nice to have another friend in the room.

CHAPTER TWELVE

Liz sat in the orange armchair by her hotel room window, looking out at the view below her. Since her room was on the fifth floor, it afforded a gorgeous view of the sweeping beach and the quaint downtown of Sea Breeze Cove. From her perch she could see the cars passing slowly down the city blocks, could see individuals like tiny dots walking along the beach, even though the water was not yet warm enough to permit swimming, except by those committed individuals who would swim even in the winter.

As Liz sat staring out at the view today, however, her gaze was glassy and unseeing. She did not notice all the little details that usually filled her with joy when she gazed out of her window. No, instead her mind was on other things. Or rather, on one person: Nadia.

Her daughter's face filled her mind, as it did so often these days. She had spent countless hours staring at the picture the private investigator had emailed to her, memorizing the contours of Nadia's face, the flecks of gold in her brown eyes, the curl of her hair. She could now, without the aid of the picture, perfectly conjure up Nadia's face, and it stayed at the forefront of her mind most of the time now.

Her phone buzzed on the wooden side table next to her chair and, though she wanted to ignore it, she realized that it might be something business-related. Sighing, she uncrossed her legs and leaned over to pick up her phone. A text from Charlotte sat on the screen and Liz tapped it to open the full message.

CHARLOTTE: Hey, Liz, just wanted to remind you that the bridal shower is today! Can't wait to see you there!

Liz groaned, setting the phone back down on the side table and turning to stare out the window once more, wrapping her arms around her as though suddenly cold. She couldn't think why she had agreed to attend the shower in the first place, but maybe if she didn't respond to the message,

Charlotte would think she hadn't seen it and she could later claim that she had forgotten about the whole thing.

The truth was that she wasn't sure she was comfortable attending the wedding shower. As welcoming as Charlotte and her friends had been in the past, they still weren't *her* friends and the prospect of making small talk with near-strangers made her feel slightly nauseous. She abhorred small talk, although years as a high-powered businesswoman had made her highly adept in social situations.

A knock at her bedroom door interrupted her thoughts and she rose from her seat, her brow furrowing as she wondered who it might be. Surely Charlotte wouldn't have gone to the trouble of also reminding her about the wedding shower in person?

Liz shuddered at the thought. Pressing one eye to the peephole in the wooden door, she looked out to see that Andy Kaplan was standing in the hallway, waiting for her to answer the door.

Liz pulled the door open, smiling at her friend somewhat distractedly. "Hi! What a surprise!" she said, her thoughts already returning to the wedding shower and whether or not she should attend. She would have to make her mind up soon or risk being late.

Andy's smile faltered and he studied her, his eyes roaming over her face. "I was going to invite you to work out with me, but I can tell something's up."

Liz furrowed her brow. "What do you mean?"

Andy gestured at her vaguely. "There's... something going on with you."

Liz raised an eyebrow. "All I said was 'Hi' and you think there's something going on with me?"

Andy laughed. "Come on, Liz, I'm getting to know you pretty well by now, and I can tell when something is on your mind. So... what is it?"

"Am I that transparent?"

"Afraid so." Andy laughed. "Well, at least to me."

Liz pulled the door open wider so that Andy could come inside her room and motioned for him to take a seat on the sturdy industrial hotel sofa. He sat down, grimacing a little.

"They sure don't make these very comfortable," he commented.

Liz smiled. "They have to make sure the sofa will last through countless guests."

"I get it, but it's still not fun to sit on. Okay, enough about the sofa. What's on your mind?"

Liz took a seat on the armchair facing him,

pursing her lips. "Well, I got invited to this wedding shower for one of my writers and her friends."

"Okay..."

"And I'm not sure whether I want to attend or not."

Andy raised an eyebrow. "That's it? It seemed like there was more going on. Come on, what aren't you telling me?"

Liz sighed. "You see right through me..."

Andy didn't respond, waiting for her to continue. Suddenly, Liz didn't think she could keep the story inside any longer.

"Years ago, when I was a much younger woman, I gave my baby girl up for adoption." She paused, holding her breath, but Andy didn't comment or look taken aback. He simply nodded for her to continue. "Since then, I've always wondered about her, but I made no effort to find her. After all, it was a closed adoption. Then, this last year, I finally hired a private investigator and he found out that she goes to college here in Sea Breeze Cove and he sent me her name and picture."

"What's her name?" Andy asked softly, as though afraid to break the flow of her words.

"Nadia. Nadia Bailey."

"Nadia," he said, turning the word over on his tongue. "That's a beautiful name."

Liz nodded. "I think so too."

"So, have you met her yet?"

"No!" Liz gulped down a deep breath. "No," she said in a quieter voice. "I haven't been able to decide whether it's the right thing to do, to be honest. Maybe she's better off not knowing who I am. Maybe I would be unwelcome, just an interruption in her life. I don't know." She paused. "The crazy thing is, I found out that she's friends with Charlotte and all of her friends."

Andy's jaw dropped. "But... that means she'll probably be at the wedding shower today."

"I know," Liz said in a low voice. "I know. I've tried to tell myself that the reason I don't want to go is that I don't want to make small talk with strangers, but the truth is that I'm terrified I'll see her there. Terrified and excited. And it just seems like maybe it might be the wrong time." She ran a hand through her hair. "Ugh, I don't know! I just don't know what to do!"

"But she's your daughter," Andy said quietly. "Don't you want the chance to talk things out with her? I'm sure she's wondered about you her whole life too."

"But I'm still so nervous," Liz said in a strangled voice.

"Liz Porter, nervous?"

Liz managed a small smile. "Yes," she admitted. "More terrified than I've ever been in my life. I just feel so alone."

Andy leaned forward then, his eyes intent and serious. "Well, you don't have to go alone. If it would help, I can come along as your date and provide you with some backup and support."

Liz blinked. "You would do that?" Her heart turned over in her chest a little at his words, the way it often did when they were together. She had to admit that she was attracted to Andy, but more than that, she was grateful for how kind he was.

"I would definitely do that. Besides, it just gives me the chance to spend more time with you," he teased, flashing her a broad smile.

Liz's heart thumped even harder and she couldn't hide her own smile. "Well, thank you. I appreciate it. And, I'm definitely going to take you up on your offer." She stood up, checking her watch and gasping at the time. "I've got to hurry if I'm going to get ready on time! Are you okay to wait here while I put on some makeup and change?"

"Absolutely. Do whatever you need to do."

Andy sat back on the sofa while Liz went to her wardrobe and picked out a nice pantsuit, which she carried into the bathroom where she changed after closing the door. It only took her a few more minutes to apply some simple yet elegant makeup and, after about ten minutes, she emerged from the bathroom, feeling shy. Andy stood up, staring at her.

"You look lovely," he said simply, giving her a small, crooked smile. He offered her his arm. "Ready to go?"

Liz nodded, unable to speak. For better or for worse, she would soon be meeting her long-lost daughter.

* * *

"Naddy! Naddy! I'm back!"

Nadia poked her head out of her bedroom to see Lainey walking toward the guest room, her hair a tangled mess and the front of her dress covered in a huge stain that looked like she had spilled juice on herself.

"What are you doing back?" Nadia asked, staring down at the little girl.

"Mommy said I was done helping."

"Is she still here?"

Lainey shook her head. "She was driving so fast!"

Nadia bit back a smile, sure that Addison was beyond stressed about the wedding shower and that Lainey spilling juice all over her outfit, necessitating a trip home, had done nothing to help the situation.

"Well, we'd better get you changed fast, because I still need to get dressed."

Lainey nodded and grabbed Nadia's hand, dragging her down the hall toward her bedroom. "Can I wear my princess dress? Daddy said we're going to play tonight. *And* he said we're going to the party!"

"Ooh, that's a lot of fun things for one night," Nadia replied, helping Lainey to take off the soiled dress and pulling a fluffy pink dress over her head. "Come on, let's brush your hair."

"Awww," Lainey complained. "It always hurts!"

"I'll be gentle, I promise."

A few minutes later, after much gentle working, Nadia had managed to get Lainey's hair somewhat under control. She checked the time on her phone and gasped, rushing back down the hall toward the guest room where she was staying. Hector would surely be arriving any minute and she hadn't even gotten dressed yet. Closing the door, she stripped off her day clothes and slid on the silky dress with a happy print of blue and purple flowers against a white backdrop. She had bought the dress just for the occasion and loved the way it looked against her tan skin. She opened the door to find Lainey waiting for her and Lainey gasped, staring up at her with wide eyes.

"You look so pretty, Naddy," Lainey breathed, her eyes enormous. "Like a princess too!"

"Thank you, sweetie." Nadia laughed, hurrying to the bathroom to check that her hair still looked good and to check that her makeup hadn't gotten smudged.

"Guess what?" Lainey cried, tagging along behind her. "Daddy said that we can have a dance party tonight after Ty goes to bed!"

"Really? That sounds perfect! You're going to have so much fun with daddy tonight, huh?"

Jesse had volunteered to stay home and watch the kids while the others were at the party, although he'd promised to bring them by for a few minutes to see everyone. Nadia checked her reflection in the mirror, satisfied that she looked nice, just as a knock sounded at the front door. Lainey took off down the hall, Nadia on her heels, to answer the door. Lainey struggled with the doorknob but managed to pull the heavy front door open.

Hector stood on the front porch, a bouquet of carnations in his hand. Lainey cocked her head to the side, seeming to size up the man on her front porch. Hector smiled down at her, pulling a single flower from the bouquet and offering it to the little girl. Lainey took it without a word of thanks, still staring up at him a little suspiciously.

"Lainey, say 'thank you'," Nadia urged, blushing a little.

Jesse came up behind them. "Hey, Hector," he called. "Here to pick up Nadia?"

"Yes, sir," Hector replied with a smile.

"Well, I hope you two have the best night," he said with a smile, all the while Lainey looked on with some suspicion.

Nadia couldn't help but smile as she stepped out onto the front porch with Hector, gratefully accepting the bouquet of flowers and sniffing them appreciatively.

"If you want, I can put them in a vase with some water," Jesse offered.

"That would be lovely, thank you," Nadia replied. She turned to Hector. "Ready to go?"

Hector nodded. "Let's do it."

Nadia was just about to pull the door shut when Lainey stuck her head out of it, glaring at Hector.

"Be nice to Naddy," Lainey warned.

"I will, I promise," Hector replied solemnly. "I will keep her safe and bring her back to you in one piece."

Lainey seemed placated by this and she finally offered Hector a shy grin. Jesse waved at them all, shooing Lainey back inside and promising to be at the party soon before closing the door behind them. Nadia took Hector's arm and they set off into the early evening sunset, ready to spend the evening with friends.

CHAPTER THIRTEEN

Sadie looked around the room, beginning to fill up with her friends and smiled to herself. Addison had worked exceptionally hard to make this wedding shower come together for Elise and Charlotte, as well as their grooms-to-be. And Addison's efforts had paid off, in Sadie's humble opinion. The room was festooned with white streamers, the balloon arch was magnificent, and the floral arrangements on the tables brought a beautiful freshness to the whole thing. Not to mention the food—the menu Addison had picked out had Sadie dying to wander over to the serving table to snag a hummus and prosciutto wrap. She was just about to do so when she felt her phone vibrating in her pocket. She pulled it out and, seeing

Ethan's name on the screen, hurried outside for some privacy.

"Ethan?" she breathed, once out on the sidewalk. The sun slanted low in the sky as the April sun headed for the horizon. "Is everything okay?"

"Hello to you too," Ethan replied from the other end of the line, his voice light and teasing. Sadie relaxed as she heard his tone. Things must be okay if he was able to talk like that.

"Hello," she teased back. "Now seriously, tell me what's going on. You've been on my mind all day."

"Well, I'm still in recovery, but every time Dr. Liang comes to check my hand, she says she's satisfied with my progress and that all signs point to the surgery having been a success!"

Sadie gasped, feeling as though she was taking the first deep breath she'd taken all day. "E, that's wonderful!"

"It is," he agreed. "I still have to do some rehab and strengthening to get back to full strength, but there's a light at the end of the tunnel now."

A couple walked past, hand in hand talking, and Sadie turned away, but not before wishing that she and Ethan were walking down the street hand in hand. She missed him so much it hurt, but he was doing what needed to be done right now, and that was what mattered.

"Do you know how long the rehab will take?"

"I'll continue doing it after I come back home, but it could be some weeks."

"That's to be expected, though, right?"

"Definitely. Now that I know I'll be back to full strength at the end of rehab, it really motivates me to give it my all. Before I had no guarantees."

"And that was so hard for you. I remember."

"You were my rock through all of that," Ethan said softly, clearly remembering the dark days after the boating accident just as Sadie was. "I wouldn't have made it without your love and patience."

"Yes, you would have," Sadie countered, her voice soft too. "You're stronger than you think, you know."

"Hey, don't discount what you did for me. You kept me going, helped me to see what I still had even though I didn't have my hand. I must have been a bear to put up with, but you did it with love and patience."

"Because I love you."

Ethan laughed softly. "I love you too."

"I can't wait until you come back home," Sadie whispered, clutching the phone more tightly to her ear, as though that would make Ethan become closer to her. "I've missed you so much."

"I've missed you too, but I'll be back before you know it."

"Promise?"

Ethan laughed. "I promise, you goose. I'm not going anywhere. Give Silver a kiss for me, will you? I've been missing him too."

Now it was Sadie's turn to laugh, which had probably been Ethan's intention. "I will," she promised. "I'd better get back to the wedding shower now."

"Oh, shoot, I forgot that was today! And here I've been monopolizing you."

"It was well worth it, love."

"I'll let you go. I love you."

"Love you too."

Sadie slid her phone back into her pocket, wrapping her arms around herself and standing on the sidewalk for a moment longer. The sky above her was streaked with the most gorgeous pinks and oranges, but all she could think about was Ethan and the call they'd just had. She was more than overjoyed for him, knowing what he had suffered when his hand had been injured, but a part of her still worried that he would come home and tell her that he no longer wanted to be part of her business.

He wouldn't say it so bluntly. No, he would find some kind explanation about why he needed to take a step back from the kennel, but the result would still be the same, and Sadie wasn't sure she could bear it. The thought of no longer working side by side with the love of her life made her unbearably sad.

No, she thought fiercely, the strong part of her taking over. *No, you're being selfish. No matter what Ethan chooses, you will support him. He would do it for you.*

And Sadie knew it was true. Ethan had been nothing but supportive of her dog-walking business from the get-go, so how could she turn around and begrudge him the chance to return to his calling as a vet if he so chose? She couldn't and she knew it. Squaring her shoulders, Sadie vowed then and there that she would support her man no matter what he chose.

* * *

"So you haven't been able to have an evening alone with Oliver since your mother came into town?"

Addison asked, shocked as she looked between
Bridget and Nina.

Nina shook her head ruefully. "Nope. It's just
been me and Mom every evening..."

Addison blew out a breath, her eyes widening
comically. "I'm sure that's been... delightful..."

The three dissolved into laughter, Nina raising
her hand to her mouth to stifle hers.

"Come on, why would you want to hang out
with your boyfriend when you can play Scrabble
with your mother?" Bridget teased, and the three
laughed even harder.

Just then, Melissa drifted by, pausing to look at
them disapprovingly. "And what is so funny?"

The three sobered instantly, although Addison
had to work to keep a straight face. "Just telling jokes
over here, that's all."

"I see." Melissa sniffed, then continued on
her way.

Addison, Nina, and Bridget looked at each other,
all on the verge of laughter once more. Addison
reveled in the moment, pleased to see that a
friendship seemed to be forming between Bridget
and Nina. Things had once been rocky there, as
Nina had tried to date Timothy, who Bridget also
liked, but things had finally gotten worked out and

everyone was with the person they were supposed to be with. It was good to see Bridget fitting in with the group. For a long time, she had been the odd one out, only there because of Elise, but everyone was starting to warm up to her, and it made Addison happy.

The bell at the front door jingled just then and Nadia and Hector walked in. Nadia, Addison noticed, was looking resplendent in her floral printed dress and there was a smile on her face that could only be the product of spending time with Hector, something that also made Addison very happy. She excused herself from Nina and Bridget and hurried over to Nadia and Hector.

"Nadia! Hector! Glad you could make it!"

"Thanks for the invitation," Nadia replied. "It looks absolutely beautiful in here, by the way. The bistro has been completely transformed."

"That was the idea," Addison said modestly. "Thank you." She turned to Hector. "Nice to see you, as always."

"Good to be here. Anything to spend some time with Nadia," Hector teased lightly, and Nadia's cheeks turned a rosy hue.

"He brought me flowers," she blurted out, looking at Addison. "A bouquet of carnations."

Addison looked at Hector with approval. "That's

a very classy move. Very gentlemanly. I have to give you kudos."

"Well, Nadia deserves the best," he said simply. He turned to Nadia. "Do you want me to get some food for us?"

"That would be great, thank you," Nadia replied, her eyes following him as he left to procure some plates of the delicious wraps and other hors d'oeuvres.

Addison smiled at Nadia, her hazel eyes warm. "It seems like things with Hector are going well," she commented.

Nadia's cheeks flushed even more, but she couldn't hide her smile. "They are," she agreed. "I really like him."

"What's not to like? The two of you are a great pair. He seems really sweet."

"He's more than sweet," Nadia said, leaning closer. "Did you know that he's been trying to help me find my birth mother?"

Addison felt her eyes widen. "Really?"

Nadia nodded. "Ever since I told him the truth about my past, he offered to help me find more information about my birth mother."

"Wow... and have the two of you found anything?"

Nadia's smile slipped and her eyes saddened as she shook her head. "No, not yet."

"I'm so sorry," Addison murmured. "That must be so disappointing. I know how much you want to find out about your birth mother."

"I do," Nadia agreed in a low voice, then she squared her drooping shoulders. "But, I'm trying to let the matter go for tonight and just enjoy the party."

"A wise decision," Addison agreed heartily. "And I think the presence of a certain handsome realtor will help you in that quest... don't you think?"

Nadia laughed behind her hand, her cheeks pink once more, but she didn't look as though she minded the teasing.

"Too true," she said, looking over to where Hector was returning with two plates of food. "Too true."

CHAPTER FOURTEEN

Liz almost turned tail and ran as Firefly Bistro came into sight. She slowed her walk, debating for the millionth time whether this was a good idea and trying to rationalize to herself that her presence would not really be missed by Charlotte. Sensing her hesitation, Andy slowed his pace too, and turned to look at her.

"Getting cold feet?" he asked.

Liz nodded. "I'm just not sure this is a good idea..."

Andy chewed the corner of his lip, thinking. Finally he said, "In a case like this, I don't think there's ever going to be a time where you feel one hundred percent ready to dive in. There will always be fear."

"I know..."

"So why put it off? You may not get another chance like this one."

Liz nodded, swallowing hard. "You're right. I just... I just need a minute to gather my thoughts."

"Take all the time you need."

Liz stared up at the darkening sky, willing herself to be brave, to take charge. She usually wasn't one to shy away from a challenge, but this was new territory for her and she couldn't help but be afraid. What if Nadia wanted nothing to do with her? Or even worse, what if Nadia wasn't even aware that she had been adopted in the first place? The thought made Liz blanch and she almost turned and sprinted down the sidewalk, but with a great effort she kept herself standing where she was. Her palms were clammy and her breath was coming in short bursts, as though she had just climbed five flights of stairs.

"Just breathe," Andy said softly, his eyes on her face. "I'll be right beside you the whole time."

Liz nodded, taking a slow inhale, holding it, and then slowly exhaling. Her heart beat slowed down a little bit, for which she was grateful. "I'm trying."

"You're doing great."

Liz raised an eyebrow and gave him a weak

smile. "We both know I'm not, but thank you for pretending."

Andy's face was serious as he gazed into her eyes. "No, I meant what I said. You're being really brave coming here tonight and the fact that you haven't run away is proof of that."

"Oh, but I've thought about it."

"But you haven't done it," Andy said firmly. "Brave."

"Thank you," Liz murmured, a surge of gratitude for his presence rushing through her. She squared her shoulders. "I think I'm ready."

"Okay then. Let's do it."

They continued walking down the sidewalk and, within a minute, were standing outside the doors. Andy and Liz both reached for the door handle at the same time, which made Liz laugh a little, the sound thin and nervous. Andy pulled open the door, holding it for Liz to walk through first. She gulped, but squared her shoulders once more and put on her best professional face.

Firefly Bistro was decorated beautifully, but it was all a blur to Liz. She stepped inside, feeling dazed and overwhelmed, unsure of where to look. If she was being honest with herself, she was afraid to look around, afraid that she would see Nadia and it would be time for her to meet her long-lost daughter. She had made it to the bistro, but she wasn't ready for the next step yet. Thankfully, someone came forward to talk to her, capturing her attention.

"You're Charlotte's agent, aren't you?" the woman asked.

Liz nodded, studying the woman, who looked remarkably like Charlotte. "And you must be Charlotte's sister, Nina."

"Correct!" Nina smiled warmly. "Thank you so much for showing up to support my sister. I know it will mean a lot to her."

"She was very kind to invite me in the first place."

"If she invited you, that means she really wants you here. I know she appreciates everything you've been doing to get her book published."

"Well, it's a good book," Liz said with a smile. "I don't foresee any major troubles finding a publisher. Your sister is a very talented writer."

"That she is. I just can't wait to see her book sitting in the display case at a bookshop!"

"That may be sooner than you think," Liz replied warmly.

An older woman who looked similar to Nina and

Charlotte stepped up to join them then, an austere expression on her face.

"Nina, do introduce me to your friend."

"Mom, this is Liz Porter. She's Charlotte's agent, remember? Liz, this is my mother, Melissa."

The austere expression vanished and Melissa leaned forward eagerly to shake Liz's hand. "Charlotte has said such wonderful things about you! It's very nice to finally meet you in person."

"Thank you. I was just telling Nina what a wonderful writer Charlotte is."

"That she is. She works so hard, my Charlotte, and she deserves to have her work published. I'm sure you're working very hard to make that happen, though."

"That I am."

"And thank you for that. I don't know if you have any children of your own, but there's nothing like the feeling a mother gets when she sees her children succeeding."

Liz felt her smile tighten and become brittle. "I'm sure it's a wonderful feeling," she managed to say. "Are you enjoying your visit to Sea Breeze Cove?"

Melissa nodded. "Visiting my daughters has been very nice. Nina's place *is* a bit cramped—I can't think why Charlotte didn't ask me to stay with her instead—but it has been very nice overall. The important thing is that I'm spending time with my daughters."

The talk of mothers and daughters hit Liz hard and she felt her hands beginning to tremble. Her nerve was beginning to fail and, just as she was thinking about spinning around and running out the door, she felt Andy's hand slip into hers, squeezing it softly. Her fingers stilled beneath his touch and she gave him a tiny smile.

"Well, it was very nice meeting you both," Liz said to the ladies. "Andy and I are going to find a seat."

Andy led her to a table in the corner and helped her to sit down. "I'm going to get us some food, if that's all right. Will you be okay on your own?"

Liz wasn't so sure, but she nodded anyway. "Thank you, that sounds wonderful."

Andy gave her an encouraging smile. "I'll be right back."

True to his word, Andy returned a couple of minutes later with two plates loaded with wraps, bacon-wrapped figs, and stuffed avocados. He set a plate down in front of Liz and then took the seat beside her. Mechanically, Liz reached for a bacon-wrapped fig and popped it in her mouth, chewing methodically although she could barely taste the food. Maybe Andy was right and everything would be okay, she thought. She was just about to reach for another bite when a woman in a floral-printed dress caught her eye.

Liz's breath caught in her throat as she saw none other than Nadia standing in a group next to a handsome young man, smiling and talking. Liz would have recognized Nadia's face anywhere, imprinted as it was in her mind. She stilled, sitting as a statue for a moment, just staring across the room at her daughter. And suddenly, in a burst of mingled fear and courage, Liz knew what she needed to do next.

* * *

"Hello, hello!" Elise called to Charlotte and Briggs as she and Gabe climbed out of their car.

Charlotte waved as Briggs called back a greeting. Elise closed the door of her car behind her and hurried over to give Charlotte and Briggs hugs, Gabe close behind her. Everyone wore huge smiles of contentment and excitement. Elise knew her face must look the same, smiling as she was and flushed with joy. She only hoped the wedding day would feel as joyful as this wedding shower already was—and they hadn't even gone inside yet.

"Ready?" Gabe asked, heading for the front door. "Ladies first!"

Elise and Charlotte grinned, linking arms as Gabe pulled open the door and let them walk through. As the two couples entered the bistro, cheers and whoops erupted all around the room, mingled with the sounds of applause and wolf whistles. Charlotte laughed and Elise blew air kisses to the whole room, waving at all of her friends. Before they could take more than a few steps into the room, they were swarmed by their friends, all reaching out to hug and kiss them, to shake hands and give high-fives, and to offer warmest congratulations.

It was many minutes later when Elise finally made her way through the crowd, flushed with happiness, to grab a cool drink of water from the open bar. She was drinking it down when Bridget approached.

"Congratulations!" Bridget exclaimed, reaching out to hug Elise.

"Thank you so much! And thank you for

everything you've done to help make this party a success. The food looks amazing."

Bridget blushed a little as she smiled. "I'll always do whatever I can for you, you know that. You gave me a second chance at life, and I don't forget it."

Elise was touched by Bridget's words, and she reached out to give Bridget another hug. "Well, you did amazingly well, and I'm so thankful for it."

Daisy bustled over then, two bottles of champagne in hand. "Let's get this party started!" she called, making the two women laugh. "Anyone want a drink?"

"I wouldn't say no to some champagne," Elise said with a grin.

Daisy poured out three champagne flutes and toasted the happy couples before polishing off her glass. Bridget took a sip of hers and then bustled off to the kitchen to carry out more trays of appetizers to replenish those that had been emptied at the food table. Daisy refilled her champagne flute and offered to top off Elise's, but Elise shook her head, laughing.

"I'm still working on the first glass, but thank you."

"You can party hard tonight, you know. It's not often you get to celebrate your engagement and your upcoming double wedding!"

"Too true," Elise agreed, taking a sip of the bubbly champagne and laughing when the bubbles tickled her nose.

"So," Daisy said, leaning forward to be heard over the hubbub in the room. "Any luck in the wedding dress department? Have you gone to any more shops?"

Elise grinned. "Actually, I think I may have finally found my perfect wedding gown."

Daisy clapped her hands, gasping. "That's amazing! I was so worried the other day when you couldn't find one that you really liked. But when do I get to see it?"

"Well, you're actually not going to see it until I walk down the aisle. No one is."

Daisy scrunched her nose and pursed her lips, looking a bit put out. "Are you sure? Not even a peek?"

"Not even a peek."

Daisy sighed but smiled. "Ah well, that only increases my anticipation for your wedding day, dear." She reached out and pulled Elise into a tight hug. "I'm just so happy for you! I knew you'd find the perfect dress in the end."

"Thank you for all your help in that department, by the way."

"Oh, it was nothing, dear. I was happy to. But, in the end, you found it all on your own."

"Hey, Daisy, how about sharing that champagne?" Arthur called from across the room, making all the guests laugh.

"Coming, coming," Daisy called back, smiling and winking at Elise.

Elise took another sip of her champagne, smiling as she watched Daisy walk across the room to Arthur. As she watched, she noticed a flash of movement as Liz wove her way through the room, making a determined beeline toward someone. Elise tilted her head to the side, her brows furrowing. She followed Liz with her eyes, her curiosity mounting as she saw Liz approaching none other than Nadia.

Why she would approach the younger woman was a mystery to Elise, but it was obvious that Nadia was the one Liz had set her sights on.

CHAPTER FIFTEEN

Nadia sipped on the club soda that Hector had thoughtfully brought over for her a few minutes previously. He had been nothing but attentive and kind, and she was glad she had invited him. The handsome young realtor was definitely finding his way into her heart and she could not deny it, even to herself. She spied him chatting with Sadie and Addison across the room and it warmed her heart further to see the way he was interacting with her friends instead of hanging back.

Swaying a little to the music, she took another drink of her club soda and scanned the room, noticing that a woman she didn't recognize was approaching her. Nadia looked around to see if the woman might be headed for someone else, but no one else was around.

She debated pretending not to see the woman, but that would be rude, so she stood her ground and let the woman step up next to her, giving her a welcoming smile. The woman, with beautiful dark skin and curly black hair, was looking slightly nervous, and Nadia wondered if it was because she didn't know many people at the party.

"How are you liking the party so far?" Nadia asked politely, when the woman didn't speak right away. "I'm Nadia, by the way."

"Nadia," the woman said slowly, as though testing how the name felt in her mouth. "Oh, I'm Liz," she added, seeming to realize that she hadn't introduced herself.

"Nice to meet you, Liz. Are you having a good time?"

Liz paused, staring into Nadia's eyes a touch too long, which made Nadia uncomfortable. "Oh, yes. It's... very good. So far, at least."

So far? Nadia wondered what she meant by that.

She looked at Liz a little more closely, noticing Liz's worried eyes and her shallow breathing, the tightness in her brittle smile. Something was definitely up with this woman, something was definitely wrong. Nadia cocked her head to the side.

"Liz," she said gently, "is everything okay?"

The older woman took a deep breath, seeming to brace herself. "Yes, I..."

Nadia waited, but nothing followed. A moment later, she heard someone calling her name from across the room. She turned her head to see Addison waving at her, beckoning her to come over.

"That's my cue," Nadia said lightly. "You'll have to excuse me, I'm so sorry."

"Oh, it's fine," Liz said in a dazed voice, still staring at Nadia in that strange way. "Don't mind me."

Nadia gave her a little wave, a little glad to get some space from Liz's intense stare. She hurried across the room to Addison's side, pausing only to drop her drink off with Hector.

"Hey, what's up?" she asked.

"I just needed some help refilling the food trays, if that's okay," Addison replied.

"That's totally fine! Happy to help."

Addison smiled at her. "Thank you so much. I can always count on you."

Nadia waved that away with a grin. "Okay, lead the way."

Addison and Nadia gathered the empty platters off the food tables and carried them into the kitchen where Bridget was already working to prepare more hummus and prosciutto wraps as well as the sandwiches of goat cheese and baby greens. A platter of bacon-wrapped figs was already ready to go back out to the serving table, which Nadia grabbed and carried out immediately. When she returned to the kitchen, she grabbed an apron, washed her hands, and joined the others assembling the wraps and sandwiches.

"I'd say the party is going really well," Nadia commented as she assembled a wrap. "Props to you," she said to Addison. "Well, both of you," she added, drawing Bridget into the conversation. "You've outdone yourself with the food."

Bridget and Addison smiled, thanking her. "It's all worth it to see how happy Charlotte and Elise are," Addison said.

"Aren't they all the cutest couples?" Bridget added.

Nadia nodded, but in truth, her mind was already back on the woman she had just met, Liz. There was something off about her, but there was also something that intrigued her and compelled her to want to know more about her. Who was she really? Why was she at the party? And above all, why had she been staring at Nadia like that?

Charlotte sipped on her champagne, watching Liz from across the room. She had been on tenterhooks when she saw Liz approaching Nadia, and had been unable to look away from their private moment, but their conversation had lasted only a few seconds before Nadia had been called away by Addison, leaving Liz standing alone and looking visibly shaken. Charlotte hurried over to her once Nadia was gone, noticing how shallow Liz's breathing was and how off she seemed.

"Liz," she said as she approached, getting her agent's attention. "Here, let's take a seat," she said, gesturing to an empty table.

Liz, moving as one sleepwalking, stumbled and sat down on one of the empty chairs, her eyes glazed as she gazed at the spot where Nadia had been standing only a minute before. Charlotte bit her lip, guilt flooding through her. It had been she who had suggested that Liz attend the party, knowing that Nadia would be in attendance. It had been she who had attempted to push Liz into meeting her long-lost daughter, without considering whether Liz or Nadia were even ready for that step. What she had done, though well meaning, was unconscionable and she was heartily ashamed of herself.

"Liz?" she asked softly, waiting until Liz finally met her eyes. "I just wanted to apologize."

"For what?" Liz asked, her brow furrowing with obvious confusion.

Charlotte took a deep breath. "For trying to force the moment with Nadia by inviting you here today. I shouldn't have meddled."

Liz simply shook her head. "I knew why you were inviting me and I still chose to come. It's not your fault."

"You did?"

Liz nodded. "It was pretty obvious."

Embarrassment flooded through Charlotte and she could feel herself blushing, but she forged on. "Well, if you're not yet ready to tell Nadia the truth about who you are and who she is, it's not too late to simply enjoy the party and wait for another opportune moment. This time on your terms and when *you* decide."

Liz blinked, then visibly relaxed against the back of her chair, blowing out a deep breath. "That would be nice. I think I like the idea of just enjoying the party and celebrating your upcoming wedding."

Charlotte relaxed a little too, seeing that Liz was truly relieved. Just then, Liz looked up, smiling at a handsome blond man who was approaching their table. He reached out and set his hand on Liz's shoulder.

"This is Andy," Liz said, introducing him to Charlotte. "He's my date tonight."

"Very nice to meet you," Charlotte said, smiling at the man and noticing how much more relaxed Liz had become since Andy had joined them. "I hope you're enjoying yourself."

"Oh, I am. By the way, congratulations on your engagement and upcoming wedding!"

"Thank you!" Just then Charlotte heard her name being called. "Oh, that's Elise. I guess it's time to open presents. Please excuse me!"

Charlotte hurried over to sit beside Elise, who was already waiting by the pile of gifts.

"Ready to get started?" Elise asked.

Charlotte rubbed her hands together comically, making the small crowd of friends watching them laugh. "Bring it on," she said. "Who doesn't love getting presents?"

* * *

Hector watched as Charlotte and Elise began opening presents. Charlotte opened a box of genuine crystal wine glasses, which made everyone ooh and ahh and Charlotte exclaimed about how she couldn't wait to host a party so she could put them to good use. Next, Elise opened a box of the same crystal wine glasses, making everyone laugh and the gift-giver exclaim about how they couldn't leave Elise out of all the fun.

Hector nursed his drink, taking another slow sip of it and drifting away from the party fun. He was something of an introvert, so being around this many people—most of them strangers—for this long was beginning to wear on him, especially because Nadia was still in the kitchen helping to prepare more food, which meant he wasn't getting to hang out with her. Not, he reminded himself, that he should begrudge her absence. It was just like her to join in and help instead of just enjoying the party. It was just one more thing he liked about her and there were so many, many things he liked about her.

One of the other guests, a handsome blond man with blue eyes, drifted over with his own drink in hand to stand near him. Hector thought he remembered the man showing up with Charlotte's agent, the beautiful black woman with the curly hair. The man turned to glance at him and they caught eyes, laughing. Hector held his drink up to toast and the man clinked his glass against Hector's.

"To the happy couples," Hector said.

"To the happy couples," the man agreed, taking a sip of his drink. "Not," he added, "that I actually know them."

Hector laughed, amused. "Hey, I don't really know them either, so we're in the same boat."

"Really?"

Hector nodded. "I just came as a plus-one to support the girl I like."

"Then we're definitely in the same boat. My date was nervous about coming tonight. I'm Andy, by the way."

"Hector. Nice to meet you."

The two men shook hands, but Hector was curious.

"Yup," Andy continued. "I met Liz at the hotel where I work."

"And you two just decided to go to a wedding shower together?"

"If it had happened like that, I can see how it would look weird," Andy admitted. "No, we met in the hotel gym and hit it off, so we've hung out a few times before this. I really like her."

"Hey, sparks can fly anywhere. No judgment. Still, it was brave of you to attend a wedding shower where you wouldn't know anyone."

"The things we do for the women we like," Andy joked, then became more serious. "Actually, it was more than that. When she told me about this shindig, she also told me about how her long-lost daughter was going to be here and she wanted to meet her, but she was nervous."

Hector felt his jaw drop. "Her long-lost daughter?"

Andy nodded. "Apparently she gave her daughter up for adoption years ago? Anyway, she's been trying to get up the courage to talk to her for ages. I don't know if she's done it yet."

"Wow... and she's sure her daughter is in Sea Breeze Cove?"

Andy nodded. "Apparently so. She hired a private investigator and everything, so I don't think there's much doubt in that department. No, she seems pretty certain that her daughter is here tonight. In fact, I think I saw them speaking a little bit ago."

Hector's whole body tensed as Andy spoke.

There was no way on earth that this was a coincidence. Liz, a woman from out of town, coming to Sea Breeze Cove of all places to find her long-lost daughter? Liz had to be Nadia's mother, especially if she came here tonight to find and talk to her daughter. There was no way it could be anyone else. No one else was young enough to be Liz's daughter except for Nadia, and now that he suspected the truth, he could see the similarities in their faces.

Liz obviously hadn't talked to Nadia yet, at least not about the truth and Hector wondered if she was actually going to. If she didn't, what should he do? On the one hand, maybe he should keep the revelation private—it wasn't necessarily his secret to tell. On the other hand, Nadia so desperately wanted to find her birth mother. Should he tell her the truth? Hector set his drink down, his mind spinning with turmoil.

CHAPTER SIXTEEN

Nadia got herself a fresh club soda then paused at the outer edge of the circle of friends, watching Charlotte and Elise finish up opening the last of their presents. Charlotte squealed with excitement as she unwrapped a gorgeous handmade wooden cutting board, perfect for arranging charcuterie boards.

"I've always wanted one that looked like this!" Charlotte exclaimed. "Thank you so much, Daisy!"

"Glad you like it," Daisy responded, taking a sip of champagne.

Nadia smiled as she watched Charlotte smooth her hand over the gorgeous wooden workmanship of the board, pleased to see how happy her friend was. With how down Nadia had been feeling lately, it was just nice to be around friends, especially for such a joyous occasion. She took a sip of her club soda, noticing suddenly that Liz was standing near her. Their conversation had been cut off before, but she had wondered why Liz had seemed so off. Now, though, Liz seemed much more relaxed as their eyes met and they both smiled.

"A happy occasion, isn't it?" Liz asked.

"Amen," Nadia agreed. "I just love weddings and everything that goes with it."

"I've been to quite a few weddings thanks to my age, but I have to agree with you—they never get old. There's just something about the way the bride and groom look at each other that makes everything all worth it."

"Oh, I know! It's not even their wedding day yet, but I've been watching Briggs with Charlotte and Gabe with Elise and those looks are already out in full force."

Liz laughed. "Well, that's because they love each other."

"As they should. They're perfect for each other."

"I'm glad to hear that. I don't really know anyone here except Charlotte."

"That's right, you're her agent, aren't you?"

"I see that word travels fast," Liz said with a grin.

Nadia shrugged, taking a sip of her club soda and

smoothing the front of her silk dress. "Well, it's a small town and it's a small friend group. Word gets around. How's her book coming?"

"Really well, thanks for asking!" Liz's eyes lit up with excitement. "Charlotte is a gifted writer and her book is coming together even better than I originally thought it would, which is saying something."

"Well, I can't wait to read it once it's been published."

"I don't think that will take very long, judging by how good this book is. I already have several interested publishers."

"That's so exciting for Charlotte," Nadia said, beaming.

Liz leaned forward conspiratorially. "And for me!"

The two women laughed and Nadia marveled at how different Liz seemed now than she had been before. She wondered once again what had been going on to make the now-relaxed woman so edgy and uptight before.

"It's so interesting that the two couples are having a double wedding," Liz commented after a moment.

"I know, it's kind of unusual."

"If it were me, I don't know if I could bear to

share the spotlight on my special day," Liz admitted with a self-deprecating grin.

Nadia pursed her lips, thinking. "I don't know... if I was really *really* close to the other couple, I think I might be okay with it, but otherwise I'm with you— why share on my special day?"

"Still, it's going to be exciting to attend a double wedding, I'm sure," Liz said. "You don't see one every day."

"That's very true," Nadia replied a bit distractedly. Near her, she had noticed that Nina was talking in a low, urgent voice to her mother. She could tell from Nina's worried eyes and creased brow that all was not well. Pausing in her conversation with Liz, she strained to hear what was going on between the mother and daughter.

"Well, think about it," Melissa was saying, her lips pinched. "I mean *you're* dating a doctor, and Charlotte has settled for a handyman? It's embarrassing for her! I think she's settling, you know. She'll regret it later, mark my words."

"Mom, please." Nina pursed her lips, glancing around. "Keep your voice down."

"And it shows," Melissa continued, as though she hadn't heard her daughter. "I mean, look at this shoddy bridal shower. It looks very thrown together at the last minute." She huffed a breath. "Nina, dear, I can only hope that your future wedding and bridal shower will be far more spectacular. Which, it will be, seeing as how you're dating a doctor."

"That's not fair." Nina made a face, looking miserable. "You shouldn't criticize Charlotte like this. She's over the moon about Briggs and he loves her more than anyone in the world. It doesn't matter what he does for work!"

Nadia knew she needed to step in. She was becoming closer with Charlotte and Nina, and she hated to see her friend suffering so. She glanced at Liz.

"You'll have to excuse me," she murmured, and the older woman nodded. Moving quickly, Nadia made her way over to Nina and Melissa.

"Isn't this wedding shower gorgeous?" she gushed, pretending she hadn't heard Melissa's earlier scathing remarks about it. She made a show of looking around appreciatively. "Addison did a wonderful job making the balloon arch and the floral centerpieces, don't you think?"

"Oh, yes," Nina agreed, relief crossing her features. "Balloon arches are much harder to make than they look."

"I know! But it was so worth it—it looks so cute! I already took a selfie with it."

"Aw, what a cute idea!"

"And the food has been so delicious," Nadia added, sighing with contentment. "Seriously, I could not get enough of those bacon-wrapped figs! I swear, I ate five or six just by myself!"

"Those *were* rather delicious," Melissa admitted, smiling a little.

"Did you try the baby greens and goat cheese sandwiches?" Nadia asked, leaning toward Melissa. "If you liked the bacon-wrapped figs, you'll like those! So delicate, but the flavor was definitely there."

"I haven't tried them, no," Melissa replied.

"You should snag one before they're gone," Nadia urged. "You don't want to miss out! Firefly Bistro is famous for its food for a reason."

"I didn't realize this bistro had such a reputation in town."

"Oh, it does," Nadia assured her. "I'm sure more than one person is sad that it's closed today for this private function."

"Oh, I'm sure," Nina agreed, giving Nadia a small smile of gratitude and Nadia grinned back at her.

"Maybe I'd better go grab a plate of food," Melissa mused. "I wouldn't want to miss out..."

"Great idea," Nina said, smiling even more widely and mouthing 'thank you' behind her mother's back to Nadia.

Nadia smiled back then, catching Hector's eye, she made her way toward him.

"Enjoying yourself?" she asked.

Hector nodded, but there was a strange look on his face. She searched his eyes, sensing in her gut that something was off. She furrowed her brow, reaching for his hand.

"Hector? What's wrong?"

Hector chewed the corner of his lip, an internal battle clearly raging inside.

"Whatever it is, you can tell me," Nadia said in a low voice, pulling him to the side so that their conversation would be more private. "I promise, you can tell me anything."

"I... Nadia, this is really important news."

"Okay..."

Hector pulled in a deep breath, his eyes meeting hers finally. "Nadia..." Again, he broke off, as though unable to find the words. Nadia's stomach clenched with anxiety.

"Just tell me," she whispered.

Hector swallowed painfully, then cleared his throat. "I don't know for certain, but all signs point to Liz Porter being your birth mother."

Nadia froze, unable to process the words. "What?" she finally choked out.

Hector nodded. "I was just talking to her date, and I think we found your mom. Apparently she's been looking for you."

Nadia reached out and grabbed Hector's arm to stay upright, she was reeling so much from the shock that she could barely stay standing. The room swam before her eyes for a moment and Hector helped her into a chair.

"I know this is a lot to take in," he said, but his words sounded distant and echoey to her.

Nadia just kept shaking her head. "It can't be," she said, over and over. "I was just talking to her a minute ago."

And suddenly, the shock began to wear off and was replaced by anger. "I was just talking to her," she repeated, more to herself than to Hector. "And she knew, and she didn't tell me?"

Shaking off Hector's hand, Nadia rose to her feet and surged across the room, making a beeline for Liz. She ignored Hector's voice behind her, her eyes locked on the woman that must be her mother. Liz turned as Nadia approached, her eyes widening as she saw the fiery look in Nadia's eyes. Her mouth dropped open a little, as though she was going to speak, but Nadia didn't give her a chance.

"I know the truth," Nadia ground out, her voice a touch too loud. A few people near them began to look over at them. "I know the truth, and you weren't the one to tell me! You should've been the one to tell me! How dare you pretend to be a stranger when you know that I'm your daughter?" Nadia demanded. "Well? What do you have to say for yourself?"

Liz blinked, gulping as her heart began to hammer. She couldn't tear her eyes away from her daughter's beautiful face, now a mask of fury. She felt tears threatening to rise to her own eyes, and she blinked again, this time more rapidly. How had Nadia found out? Tearing her eyes away from Nadia, she glanced over at Andy, who was grimacing.

"I'm so sorry," Andy murmured. "I was talking to Hector and since I had no idea that he was connected to Nadia, I told him everything."

"You told him?" Liz breathed, barely able to form the words. She was keenly aware that more and more eyes were starting to look over at the altercation, though thankfully not everyone had noticed yet.

"Well?" Nadia demanded again, forcing Liz to look at her again. "What do you have to say for yourself?"

Liz bit her lip, searching herself frantically for words. "I... years ago, I gave my daughter up for adoption. It was a closed adoption, so I didn't know what had happened to her. Recently, I hired a private investigator to find her and based on what he found, I came to Sea Breeze Cove. Nadia, I think you're my daughter."

Nadia's eyes brimmed with unshed tears as an expression of hurt and anger took the place of her righteous indignation. "How could you not tell me?"

Liz stared into her daughter's eyes, frozen and unable to speak. Andy stepped up beside her, wrapping his arm protectively around her shoulders, offering her silent support as the tension filled air between Liz and Nadia thickened. Liz felt nauseous and the room began spinning around her a little. She leaned into Andy's side embrace, needing him to keep her on her feet. None of this was going the way she had wanted it to, and looking into her daughter's tear-filled eyes, she could see that Nadia felt the same way.

CHAPTER SEVENTEEN

Nadia's fists were clenched tightly at her sides and her whole body was taut with tension as she glared into her mother's eyes, waiting for an answer. None came. Nadia's chest rose and fell in heaving, jerky motions as her breath hitched over and over. Liz met her gaze, and Nadia saw her swallow convulsively. Her eyes drooped with sadness and anxiety that tugged at Nadia's heart until she steeled herself against it, reminding herself that Liz had essentially lied to her by not telling her the truth immediately.

Liz swallowed again, then cleared her throat. "Nadia, I... I can explain..."

"Really." Nadia scoffed, making it a statement and not a question.

"I..." Liz clutched at Andy's free hand, obviously

needing his support. Again, Nadia felt a twinge of guilt, but she shoved it ruthlessly aside.

"Well?" Nadia demanded. "Spit it out."

She heard gasps around her but she didn't tear her eyes away from Liz, who was looking crumpled and broken, supported by Andy so that she could remain standing. Liz took a deep breath, closing her eyes for a moment and seeming to gather the strength to speak. When she finally did, her voice was low and pleading.

"I was so young when I got pregnant with you, and I... I wasn't ready for a baby yet. The father had left and it would have been just me trying to raise a baby on my own, and I just couldn't."

Nadia didn't lower her glare for an instant. Liz blew out a breath and continued on.

"You have to understand that even though I gave you up for adoption, I loved you already. I didn't think that I could do the best job of raising you all by myself. I knew deep in my heart that I wasn't prepared to be the kind of mother that you would need, so I gave you up to a wonderful family. The kind of family you deserved to have all along."

Nadia folded her arms more tightly, biting the inside of her cheek to keep her chin from trembling as new tears threatened to rise just below the surface.

"And now look at you," Liz said softly, her face softening, becoming even more vulnerable. "You've clearly grown into a lovely, capable woman. And I'm so glad, so very, very glad about that." Liz reached up and wiped away a tear that had spilled out and run down one of her cheeks. "That being said, I would love to get to know that lovely, capable woman better." She paused, her eyes beseeching as they searched Nadia's. "I just want the chance to make things right, to get to know my daughter for the first time," she whispered, her voice breaking.

Nadia could feel her reserves of angry strength beginning to crumble, and she clutched at them for dear life. Liz's words had pierced her to her core, had made her heart ache for what the woman must have gone through all those years ago and ever since, but she shoved those feelings aside. She was too wound up emotionally, too confused and conflicted to take pity on her mother.

"Well, then, why did you spend so long staying away from me, huh?" Nadia exploded. "If you really missed me that much, why didn't you find me sooner? Or why didn't you come see me the minute you knew who I was?"

Liz flinched at the venom in Nadia's voice, but she didn't look away from Nadia's fiery gaze.

"You have to understand," Liz said pleadingly, "I was hardly capable of raising a child at that time, especially by myself. I knew I had to give you up for your own good. And, for your own good, I thought a clean break would be best. I didn't want you to be weighed down and confused by me. I wanted you to focus on your adoptive family." She gulped and wiped at more tears that cascaded down her cheeks. "I promise you, I wasn't trying to hurt you. I never wanted to hurt you. I just wanted to do right by you. I was doing what I thought was best."

"And what about now? Why didn't you come find me sooner?" Nadia demanded.

"I..." Liz sighed, the sound of a broken woman. "I was a coward," she whispered. "I wasn't sure that you would even want to meet me. Again, I wanted to do right by you and I didn't know what the right path was for you and for me."

Nadia's chest ached and she realized she was holding her breath. She let it out in a slow sigh as she gazed at Liz's tear-stained face. A growing part of her was softening toward her mother, and was beginning to see the agonizing decision Liz had made all those years ago. That part of her was tempted to rush to her mother and wipe away her tears, enfold her in an embrace, and tell her that it was going to be okay.

But she wasn't ready. Not yet.

Suddenly the room felt too hot for Nadia. She could feel everyone's eyes on her, waiting for her to speak, but she didn't know what to say. The worst of her anger had blown away, leaving her feeling vulnerable and defenseless. Worst of all, Liz—her birth mother—stood waiting for an answer too. An answer Nadia wasn't sure how to give, an answer she hadn't even found for herself yet. Panic bubbled in her stomach and she suddenly knew that she needed to get away from all the eyes, from all the tension in the room. Without a word, she turned on her heel and plunged through the crowd of people, racing for the front door of the bistro.

She pushed through it, stumbling as she ran down the sidewalk in her high heels and shivering a little in the cool night air. She wasn't sure where she was going, but all she knew was that her mind was screaming *away, away, away.* She heard someone call her name but she didn't look back as she continued to hurry down the sidewalk, heading nowhere fast. A moment later, she heard the sound of running footfalls and then a hand grabbed her arm.

"Nadia, wait!"

Nadia slowed, recognizing Hector's voice. He tugged gently on her arm, pulling her to a stop.

When she finally turned to face him, her eyes downcast, he silently pulled her tightly against him in a warm embrace, holding her as her shoulders began to shake and the tears she had been holding back began to flow freely. In the warm circle of his arms, Nadia cried, the sobs racking her body and her tears staining the front of his shirt. She had no words, only tears. Shock still coursed through her—she had gone from wanting to find her birth mother to suddenly realizing the very woman had been in town for weeks. All of it left her off balance, feeling angry at the woman who had had a chance to tell her the truth but had hidden it for weeks, but also sad for the time lost and sad for the woman who had felt she had no choice but to give her baby away.

"Shh, shh…" Hector whispered, rubbing her back in slow circles and swaying gently. "I've got you."

Nadia wiped at her eyes. "What do I do?" she whispered. "How can I ever forgive her?"

Hector wiped at a tear that Nadia had missed and pressed a gentle kiss to her forehead. "Well, it seems like she wants to make amends. Maybe eventually you'll be able to let her."

Nadia tensed, but Hector held her more tightly.

"Hey, hey, I'm not trying to tell you what to do. I want you to know that I'm on your side in all of this, okay? Whether you choose to give your birth mother a chance or not, you have my full support."

Nadia relaxed in his arms, resting her now-aching head against his chest. "Thank you," she murmured into his shirt. Suddenly she felt overwhelmingly and achingly exhausted. "I think I just want to go home."

"Okay then," Hector said simply. "Let's get you home then."

And with that, he took her hand and began walking her back to his car, Nadia following meekly and trying to focus only on his hand holding hers and the fact that soon she would be wrapped up in bed, hopefully able to sleep and forget all of this, at least for a while.

Sadie looked around at the crowd of her friends, seeing the shock and tension that she herself felt reflected on all of the faces around her. Beside her, Charlotte and Briggs were leaning against one another, Charlotte looking utterly stunned. Across the room, Addison had her hand over her mouth, tears running silently down her cheeks. Most of the other guests simply looked uncomfortable, unsure of where to look or what to do. After Nadia raced out, Liz collapsed into a chair, the man with her holding her hand and rubbing her back slowly. Quiet conversations broke out around the room as the guests whispered about what had just happened. Sadie didn't want to do that, though. She didn't want to rehash the awful scene that had just occurred or talk about what Nadia and Liz were going to do.

Slipping away from the crowd, she slid her phone out of her pocket and slipped into the kitchen to call Ethan. There was only one person she wanted to talk to at the moment, and that was her boyfriend. Finding the kitchen deserted, Sadie leaned against a stainless steel prep surface and clicked on Ethan's contact in her phone, holding the phone up to her ear. It rang three times and then Ethan's warm voice answered at the other end of the line.

"Hey, babe."

"Hey," she replied, already relaxing a little with the sound of his voice in her ear.

"I thought you were going to be at the wedding shower?"

"I am, I just took a moment away to call you."

Ethan chuckled softly. "Well, I'm honored. Sorry I couldn't be there with you, and I'm sorry I haven't been there to help you work on the business."

At the mention of their business, Sadie stiffened a little, blinking back tears as she silently wondered if he would ever actually work on the business with her ever again. She sniffed quietly, reminding herself that even if their future working together would be over, she was going to be happy for him no matter what he decided.

"It's okay. What you're doing is the most important thing right now."

"Well, I promise I'll be home soon, okay?"

"I can't wait for that, to be honest. I've missed you so much, even though it's only been a few days."

"I've missed you too," Ethan replied, his voice caressing her. "Now, tell me about the wedding shower. What did I miss?"

Sadie gave a mirthless laugh. "Well, you actually missed quite a bit. It turns out Nadia—you remember Nadia, Addison's nanny?"

"I do."

"Well, it turns out that she was adopted, and her birth mother came to the wedding shower and Nadia found out who she was."

"Who was it?"

"Liz Porter, Charlotte's agent."

Ethan sucked in a breath. "No way. Was it at least a beautiful reunion?"

"Not even a little bit." Sadie squeezed her eyes shut, shaking off the tension that filled her at the memory. "There was a big scene. Nadia was really angry and she ended up storming out."

"Oh my goodness…"

"It was awful. I don't know what's going to happen now."

"Well, I'm even more sorry I wasn't there to support you," Ethan said softly. "I know how much you hate conflict, and it sounds like it was a bad one. I wish I could've been there to give you emotional support."

Sadie gave a small smile, even though he couldn't see it. "I wish you could've been here too, but knowing how much you care about me is already helping me to move past it." She sighed. "I'm not sure things with Nadia and Liz will be okay, but as for me, I'm fine. I've got everything I need, including a wonderful man who loves me."

"I don't know about 'wonderful'," Ethan laughed, "but I do love you very much."

"Well, come home soon, okay? I miss you."

"I'll be home before you know it. Love you."

"Love you too."

Sadie slid the phone back into her pocket, feeling relieved to have talked to Ethan and more relaxed now that she had done so. Peeking back into the main room of the bistro, she could see that things had returned to a semi-normal state. Liz and her date had left and the others were mingling and talking, trying to revive the fun spirit that had been shattered by the altercation. Taking a deep breath, Sadie planted a smile on her face and returned to try and enjoy the rest of the party.

CHAPTER EIGHTEEN

A few days had passed since the disastrous bridal shower and Nina and Melissa had come over to visit Charlotte in her home. Nina walked arm in arm with her mother down the sidewalk toward Charlotte's house, basking in the soft April sunshine and talking about how nice it was to only need a light jacket.

"Sea Breeze Cove really shines at this time of year," Nina said as they turned up the footpath that led to Charlotte's front porch. "It's lucky for you that you get to be here around this time of year."

"Indeed," Melissa agreed, raising her hand to knock on Charlotte's door.

Charlotte answered a moment later, wearing comfy joggers and a light sweatshirt, which Nina noticed Melissa immediately noticing and frowning about. Nina hurried to greet her sister before their mother could say anything about Charlotte's casual attire.

"Hey, Char," she said, reaching over to hug her sister. "Is now a bad time?"

"No, it's actually perfect," Charlotte replied. "I was just taking a break from writing and would love some company. Come on in."

Nina and Melissa stepped inside the house and Charlotte shut the front door behind them.

"Can I get you some coffee?"

"None for me, thank you," Melissa said, "but I'm sure Nina would love some."

"I would," Nina agreed.

"Nina, why don't you help me make the coffee? Mom, would you like to take a seat in the living room? We'll be just a minute."

"Don't mind if I do," Melissa said, sinking into an armchair by the front window that afforded a view of the beach and immediately settling in.

Nina and Charlotte walked down the hall to the cozy kitchen, where Charlotte turned on her coffeemaker.

"So," Nina said, leaning forward and searching her sister's eyes. "How have you been since the bridal shower? Things... did not go as planned."

"You can say that again," Charlotte said with a sigh. "I can't think of a worse way for the shower to end, and to think that I orchestrated the meeting! I was the one that invited Liz, knowing that Nadia would be there. It's all my fault. I shouldn't have meddled."

Nina frowned, hugging her sister. "You didn't mean for any of that to happen. You were trying to do a good thing."

"I was, but look how it turned out."

"I know..."

Charlotte sighed again. "I spoke with Liz after the shower, and she's still really upset and shaken up. I feel so bad for what I put her through. She should've been allowed to decide the timing of when, or even if, she made contact with Nadia." She rubbed at her eyes and then ran a hand through her hair, frowning when she hit a tangle and working it loose before looking at Nina. "I feel bad for Nadia too. I mean, her whole world changed in the space of a moment, and now she has to deal with what she's learned."

"Maybe now that everything is out in the open, some healing will actually happen. Maybe what happened at the shower is actually a good thing,"

Nina commented, pulling some mugs from the cabinet for their coffees.

"Maybe." Charlotte bit her lip. "I invited both Nadia and Liz to the wedding," she admitted. "Maybe they can resolve things at the reception or something. I don't know."

Nina gasped. "Are you sure that's a good idea? Do they both know the other will be there?"

"I think so, so it's really up to them to decide if they attend or not."

"Well," Nina said slowly, thinking through the problem, "then maybe you're right. Maybe they'll work through something."

Footsteps sounded in the hallway and, a moment later, Melissa entered the kitchen. "What's taking so long? I've been waiting forever."

"Coffee takes a bit of time," Nina pointed out.

Melissa ignored that, turning to Charlotte. "I just want you to know, dear, that I approve of Briggs," she said, her voice somewhat condescending, although Nina could tell that her mother meant it kindly.

"Thank—" Charlotte began, but Melissa cut her off.

"Of course, Nina is the one making the brilliant match since she found a doctor," Melissa continued, smiling at Nina with approval. "Now, that's a proper vocation for a young man. Not this... handyman business."

Nina frowned, her insides squirming. "I know you mean that as a compliment toward Oliver," she said, trying to keep her voice even. "But I don't appreciate you putting Briggs down in the process."

Melissa looked affronted, her eyes widening. "What are you talking about? I'm not dismissing Briggs by any means. I was simply complimenting your young man. And, of course, I do hope that your wedding will be far grander when you get married. None of this casual beach affair."

Charlotte frowned. "A simple wedding is what I wanted. This is going to be a special day for me."

"I'm sure it will," Melissa said somewhat dismissively, looking at the coffee pot, which was still only half full. "Ah, the coffee isn't ready yet. I'll go back to my chair in the living room to wait."

Without waiting for a reply, their mother turned and walked back down the hallway. A moment later, Nina heard Melissa taking her seat in the living room by the window. The two sisters turned to look at one another and, as one, they sighed and rolled their eyes.

Nina spoke in a low voice, quiet enough that their mother wouldn't hear. "When is she going to understand that we each deserve to be happy on our own terms, and that it doesn't have to meet with her approval to be right for us?"

"I don't know that she ever will," Charlotte admitted, leaning against the kitchen counter. "Don't worry about me, though. I know how she feels about Briggs versus Oliver, and I don't mind. I know in my heart that Briggs is the man for me, and I couldn't be happier."

Nina smiled, relieved, and returned the hug Charlotte reached out to give her. Their relationship with their mother had gone through several ups and downs, and even though they understood Melissa better now thanks to the journal Charlotte had uncovered at their aunt's house, things were still far from perfect. Dealing with Melissa's critical attitude wasn't always a walk in the park, but Nina was grateful that she and her sister had always had each other's backs because of it.

"Well, I'm happy for you too," Nina said as Charlotte poured her a mug of coffee. "Briggs is perfect for you and I can see how happy he makes you."

"Thanks! Your support means everything, especially since I don't really have Mom's."

"Well, you'll *always* have mine," Nina replied, smiling warmly. She headed toward the hallway, giving her sister a wink and whispering, "Now, shall we go and face the dragon?"

Charlotte laughed as she followed her sister down the hallway to sit with their mother.

Elise's nerves had been jangling for days following the scene at the bridal shower. The whole disastrous scene had come out of the blue for her—she had had no idea that Nadia was adopted, nor that Liz was Nadia's birth mother. The whole thing had been heartbreaking and unsettling in the extreme, and Elise still hadn't quite recovered from it all.

"Elise? Are you all right?"

Elise looked up from her computer in the office at Firefly Bistro to see Bridget standing in the doorway.

"What?"

"Are you all right?" Bridget repeated, looking concerned. "You haven't moved a muscle in ages and you look... upset."

Elise sighed, getting up from her desk. "Maybe I just need to take a break from spreadsheets for a minute."

"Always a good idea. You can help me roll utensils into napkins," Bridget joked.

"Honestly, that sounds like a good distraction right about now," Elise admitted. "Lead the way."

"Oh, you don't actually have to—"

"No," Elise said firmly. "I really want to."

A moment later the two friends stood side by side at the stainless steel prep counter and Elise reached for a stack of clean napkins and began rolling a fork, knife, and spoon into the top napkin, then set the finished bundle aside.

"Work like this soothes me," she said, reaching for another napkin.

"Me too."

"You know, it was more than just the spreadsheets that was upsetting me," Elise said.

"I thought it might be."

"I was thinking about everything that happened at the wedding shower."

"It's been on my mind too," Bridget said, setting aside a finished utensil bundle. "Can you believe what happened? It was crazy."

"Crazy is an understatement." Elise blew out a breath. "I have a confession... seeing so many relationships plagued with drama has given me a small case of cold feet. I mean," she rushed to add, seeing the shock on Bridget's face. "If a relationship can fall apart so quickly, what guarantees do I have that *my* relationship with Gabe won't fall apart too?"

Bridget gave her a sympathetic look, reaching out and touching her arm lightly. "Okay, the shower was a bit of a disaster, no one is denying that. But here's the thing—that has nothing to do with your wedding. It wasn't an omen, it wasn't a sign of disasters to come. Your wedding is going to be amazing."

"Yes, it will be," a voice said behind them.

Both women turned around to see that Arthur had entered the kitchen unbeknownst to them and he was looking concerned.

"My dear, I had no idea you were feeling so worried, but you have no reason to be," he said, taking his daughter's hand.

Elise sighed. "Logically, I know you're right and that I'm being unreasonable, but I can't stop having some wedding jitters. Gabe and I have been so happy lately—are we risking that happiness by getting married? What if it's the wrong step? Was the wedding shower falling apart a sign of bad things to come?"

"Didn't you hear what I just said?" Bridget asked with a little laugh. "Come on, the wedding shower wasn't an omen!"

Arthur nodded then reached out to hug his daughter. "Bridget is right. The wedding shower was *not* an omen. And as for your worries about moving forward in this next step with Gabe, I don't think you need to be."

"How can you be so sure?"

Arthur sighed. "My dear, I know I had some... reservations... about Gabe in the past, but the past few months he has proved, over and over again, that he is a wonderful young man. As your father, I fully support this union. I don't think you could find a more loving husband than Gabe."

Elise nodded, touched to her core to hear her father saying such supportive things about her fiancé. She thought about the upcoming wedding, picturing her standing on the beach next to Gabe and excitement flared in her belly at the thought. Just because they were officially tying the knot didn't mean that anything would change between the two of them—if anything, they would only come to love one another more.

"You're both right," Elise finally said, nodding slowly. "Gabe is the one for me, and I want nothing more than to be his wife. I'm confident that our relationship is strong enough to stand the test of time."

"That's the spirit!" Arthur said, patting her on the back and turning to leave. "I'm proud of you, dear."

"Thanks, Dad."

"I'm proud of you too," Bridget said as they returned to folding utensils into napkins. "I mean, I know you don't need my stamp of approval, but you have it."

"Thanks," Elise responded with a laugh. "It does mean a lot."

The two continued working, folding knives, forks, and spoons into napkins while they talked and laughed. But, as they worked, Elise still worried about something else. Visions of torn dresses, of wine spilled on white fabric, of torrential rain opening up during the beachside ceremony, of another bitter and public altercation opened up before her mind's eye and she shivered. If the wedding shower could fall apart so spectacularly, with no warning, who was to say that the upcoming wedding wouldn't be plagued with even more disasters?

CHAPTER NINETEEN

"Thanks for bringing breakfast over," Sadie said, popping the last bite of quiche into her mouth. "I really appreciate it! You didn't have to do that. Really, you should be resting."

"It's just my hand that is healing," Ethan said with a laugh. "Not my whole body. I'm perfectly capable of picking up breakfast."

"Well, you did a great job picking it out! This quiche is amazing." Sadie patted her full belly. "Two slices was a little too much but I just couldn't help myself."

"Two slices was the perfect amount. You've got to keep your strength up to work on the kennel. Speaking of, are you sure I can't come help you with it today?"

"No, I'm sure," Sadie promised. "What if you injured your hand again? We can't have that. Stay here and rest up. Besides, Addison is coming over to help, so I'm good."

"What are you working on today?"

Sadie stood and began clearing up her dirty dishes, taking them to the sink. "We're deep cleaning the whole house and then, if we have time, we're putting together some storage cabinets from IKEA."

"Sounds like a full day." Ethan rose too, and wrapped his arms around Sadie's waist. "I'm so proud of how much you've accomplished."

"Well, there's still a ton to do..."

"Don't discount what you've already done."

"Thanks, babe." Sadie checked her watch and gasped. "I better run. Addison will probably be waiting for me already and I have the keys to the house."

Sadie quickly kissed Ethan goodbye, pausing to kiss his healing hand as well, and then threw on a light jacket and rushed to grab her keys and head out the door. She was soon in the car heading out into the bright May sunshine and over to the house. As she had worried, when she got there, Addison was already waiting for her on the front porch, Lainey in

195

195

tow. Sadie hopped out of her car and hurried up the front steps to them.

"Sorry I'm late," she called.

Addison waved that off. "You're totally fine. Lainey and I have just been playing a game of I Spy while we waited."

"It was so fun!" Lainey cried, beaming. "I won three times!"

"That's awesome," Sadie replied with a laugh. She fitted the key into the lock and let them all into the house. "Oh, I forgot the cleaning supplies in the trunk of my car. I'll be right back."

Sadie hurried back down the steps and popped open the trunk of her car, lugging in some cleaning buckets, mops and brooms, and some other cleaning supplies.

"Where's Silver?" Lainey asked as Sadie set down her supplies.

"Silver is a big help, usually," Sadie laughed, "but I didn't think he'd be too good at cleaning. Not like you, huh?"

"I'm really good at mopping. Mommy said so." Lainey puffed out her chest proudly and Sadie tousled her curls.

"I'll bet you are."

"Here, sweetie, can you start wiping the

baseboards? Like this?" Addison said, showing her daughter how to do it. "All the baseboards in the whole house need to be cleaned."

"I can do it!" Lainey promised, her face set in serious lines as she began to work.

Once she was absorbed in her task, Addison drew close to Sadie. "I'm so sorry, I know I probably shouldn't have brought her, but I was trying to ease the load for Nadia today. She's been under a lot of strain."

"It's not a problem, seriously. Don't give it another thought."

Addison looked relieved. "Thanks."

"Besides, she's already proving to be a huge help."

"Well," Addison said with a laugh. "We'll see how long it lasts before she gets bored."

"Whatever she does for us is just a bonus then," Sadie said lightly, grabbing a broom and beginning to sweep.

She had only been sweeping for a couple of minutes when she heard a light knock at the front door. Furrowing her brow in confusion, Sadie set the broom aside and headed to the front door. She pulled it open to see Ethan's old receptionist from his veterinary office standing at the front door.

"Carolyn!" Sadie said, smiling warmly. "What a nice surprise!"

"I hope I'm not interrupting," Carolyn replied with a smile. "I've just been to see Ethan and I wanted to stop by and see the progress on your kennel."

"Well, come on in! There's not a whole lot to see yet. We're just cleaning today."

Carolyn stepped inside, looking around the large front room. "There's good natural light in here. It's the perfect space for what you have planned."

Sadie gave Carolyn a quick tour of the rest of the house, showing her where everything would go and what the vision was. Carolyn oohed and ahhed in all the right places, making Sadie feel good about her business plans. When Carolyn was about to leave, they paused for a moment.

"It's a miracle about Ethan's hand, you know," Carolyn said, one hand on the front door's knob. "I'm so happy for the both of you."

"Thank you," Sadie replied. "We're both overjoyed that he was able to find a specialist that could work that miracle for him."

"I do miss working for him and seeing the both of you more often."

An idea occurred to Sadie—should she offer

Carolyn a job at her kennel? Carolyn would be enormously helpful. But... what if Ethan was planning to reopen his veterinary practice? She sighed internally, realizing she would be jumping the gun by offering a job when she wasn't sure of Ethan's plans yet.

"Well, I'll see you soon," Carolyn was saying, pulling Sadie back from her thoughts.

"Absolutely! We'll see you at the wedding soon."

"Bye now!"

Carolyn pulled the door closed behind her and Sadie turned to pick up her broom again but saw that Addison had already finished sweeping and mopping all the rooms while she had been giving the tour. A sad mood had settled over Sadie in the wake of Carolyn leaving. It just brought back all the questions of what Ethan would do when his hand had fully healed. Sighing, Sadie began opening a box that held the pieces for one of the storage cabinets as Addison returned from mopping one of the back rooms.

"Sadie?" Addison said, noticing the sad expression on Sadie's face. "Is everything okay?"

Sadie began pulling pieces out of the box, hunting for the directions. "Everything is fine, why?"

Addison gave her a piercing look. "Come on, I know you better than that. What's on your mind?"

Sadie blew out a breath, smiling in spite of herself. "I never could hide anything from you."

"Quit stalling," Addison replied with a laugh. "What's wrong?"

Sadie drilled a screw into place before answering. "I'm still thinking about Ethan," she finally admitted. "I'm so happy that his surgery was a success, but if he goes back to being a vet, I would miss working with him so much."

"I know," Addison said softly. Her eyes brightened. "Hey, I just had an idea! If he does re-open his veterinary practice, it's highly possible that he might send more business our way. In a way, it could be a great business opportunity for us."

"That's a good way of looking at the upside," she agreed, grateful for her friend's positivity. "Come on, let's get this cabinet built."

As they worked, Addison continued to try and cheer her up, and Sadie tried to pretend to be happy. Deep down, though, she continued to worry about what Ethan would choose. She would support him no matter what, and she knew he would always do the same, but Sadie wished with all her heart that he would still choose to work side by side with her in their business venture.

They had been great partners so far and she truly wanted to continue working with him. It wasn't everyone that got to spend their days with the loves of their lives, working side by side, and she had been blessed to experience that. And, if she was being honest with herself, she just wasn't ready to let that go. Selfish or not, Sadie wanted Ethan by her side.

"Nadia? Where are you?" Addison called into the quiet house.

"I'm just in Tyler's room, changing his diaper," Nadia called back.

Addison had just taken Lainey out for a mother-daughter date to the library to pick out new books for Lainey to enjoy. She set the bag of books on the floor in the living room and Lainey dived into it, eagerly pulling picture books from the bag and beginning to pore over them. Addison smiled at the sight, then headed down the hallway to Tyler's room, where Nadia was just buttoning up Tyler's onesie. Tyler squealed with delight when he saw his mother, waving his arms in the air for her. Addison walked over and picked him up as Nadia threw away the dirty diaper.

As she bounced Tyler gently, Addison watched Nadia. Nadia looked downcast and worried, as she had ever since the disastrous wedding shower. She knew that Nadia was still grappling with everything that had happened, but she hadn't talked about it yet, at least not with Addison. Knowing that it was time, Addison led Nadia to the living room and they sat on the sofa together, Tyler already falling asleep in Addison's arms.

"We should talk about it, you know," Addison said softly.

"Talk about what?"

"Come on," Addison said, giving Nadia a look. "I know you know what I meant. We should talk about what happened at the wedding shower."

Nadia toyed with the fringe on one of the throw pillows, pulling it into her lap and hugging it for support. "It was awful," she finally said, her voice strained. "I mean... how could she not find me sooner? How could she just pretend to be a stranger when she knew I was her daughter?"

"I know," Addison replied, her voice gentle. "I can't imagine what that feels like." She paused.

"Does it help at all that now you at least know who your birth mother is?"

Nadia shrugged. "I thought it would help, but I just don't know yet."

"Maybe it would help to calm the waters in your soul if you actually talked to Liz," Addison pointed out cautiously, waiting to see if Nadia would blow up at the suggestion. When nothing happened, Addison continued. "After all, no good can come of just stewing about it all. She's the one that has answers and maybe if the two of you talk you'll come to understand one another better."

"I know you're probably right," Nadia began, her voice hesitant. "Part of me wants to get to know her better, but..." she sighed, tears rising in her eyes. "It was just a lot, you know? I didn't expect meeting my birth mother to be so emotionally complicated, nor did I expect to meet her the way it all went down. It came out of nowhere and, if I'm being honest, it hurt more than I expected it to. After all, I was meeting the woman who chose not to raise me. She gave me away, like I didn't even matter!"

Addison's heart ached as she listened to Nadia. She sighed deeply. "Oh, Nadia..." She paused, searching for the right words. "I know what it's like to have a child," she said softly. "You can't imagine the love that poured over me when I held them in my arms for the first time."

"But if she loved me, why let me go?"

"That's what I was getting to," Addison said firmly. "Even though I loved them so much, raising them has been incredibly hard. Even with Jesse by my side, raising children in a two parent household is still hard. We've still needed to reach out for help, like asking you to nanny, on more than one occasion. It sounds like Liz didn't have *anyone* to lean on. I can't even imagine how insanely hard it would be to raise a child alone. Honestly, she was probably doing right by you to give you to a family better equipped to raise you."

Nadia sat quietly, seeming to process Addison's words. A tear slid down her cheek. Heart aching, Addison reached over and hugged Nadia.

"I know it's hard, but Liz has given you the gift of the truth—now you know who your birth mother is. It's up to you to accept that gift and try to get to know her better. But that's fully up to you."

"Thank you," Nadia whispered, wiping at her eyes. "I don't know what I would do without your kindness."

"I'm always here for you, I hope you know that." Nadia nodded. A thought occurred to

Addison. "How are things going with your adoptive parents?"

Nadia bit her lip. "I've been talking to them more lately, trying to mend fences a bit."

"'That's wonderful! How has that been going?"

"It's been hard," Nadia admitted. "I've had to overcome my fears and just be really honest with them. I told them that I've hated being caught in the middle of their divorce and that it hasn't been fair to me or Samuel."

"And what did they say?"

"I think they took it to heart. They've been acting a bit kinder to each other and not trying to get me to pick sides so much anymore. I'm really happy about that." She sighed. "Honesty and facing things head on seem to have helped and honestly... maybe that's what needs to happen between me and Liz."

Addison squeezed Nadia's knee sympathetically. "I think that's really wise."

"It's just so hard feeling like my family is splintered and now I have a new 'splinter' to add to it all."

"I know..." Addison smiled at Nadia. "Just remember, family is about more than blood, and you've got a huge family of friends that are all rooting for you, including me and Jesse. We've got your back, okay? Remember that."

Nadia smiled gratefully, fresh tears rising to her eyes. "Thank you. You have no idea what that support means."

Words failed her and all Addison could do was enfold Nadia in another hug.

CHAPTER TWENTY

Ethan breathed deeply of the fresh, early spring air. He loved this time of year with all of the plants and flowers coming into bloom, awakening after the darkness of winter. He found himself smiling as he drove with the windows down toward the kennel, luxuriating in the beauty of the day. Through the windshield and the windows, he had perfect views of Sea Breeze Cove coming back to life in more ways than one. Now that the weather was warming up, children played in yards and couples went for walks. The beach looked more inviting than ever as the vista opened up when he crested a hill. Ethan marveled at the view, pausing for a few extra moments at a stop sign to take it in.

Man, I'm so lucky to live here, he thought.

There's nowhere else I'd rather be, and nowhere else where spring looks so perfect.

If he was being honest with himself, he knew that, despite his love of spring, the real reason he was so chipper was his hand—it was healing quickly from the surgery and the tremors and stiffness that had plagued him for so long were disappearing, which meant he would have full use of his hand again. Ethan shuddered, remembering those dark, dark days after the accident, when it seemed like his whole world had crashed and burned and fallen apart. He had not been able to see back then how he would go on. The thought of not being a vet had crushed him, making it feel as though he was swimming through darkness most days. Ethan shook his head, pushing away the dark remembrances.

As he parked, Ethan gazed down at his healing hand, awe filling him as he did so. It still blew his mind that Dr. Liang had been able to work miracles on his hand, restoring full range of motion and steadiness to it. It was life-changing and he hadn't felt this happy in a long time. Sure, he had eventually found happiness after the accident, making peace with his injured hand and that his life would look differently than he had expected. That was mostly thanks to the enduring love of Sadie, who had not given up on him even when he had battled with a deeper depression and anger than he had ever known. Again, he shuddered at the memories, but gratitude for Sadie and all of her sacrifices for him also filled his heart. He looked down at his hand again, flexing the fingers and stretching them out again. Now that he had received the surgery, he was more than just accepting life, he was relishing it!

Whistling to himself, Ethan climbed out of the car and closed the door behind himself, stretching and breathing in the crisp air. Now that his hand was on the mend, he had discovered more than just joy— he had found some much-needed clarity about his future and what he wanted it to look like. Still whistling a jaunty tune, Ethan headed up the front steps and opened the front door of the kennel. The sounds of hammering greeted him, which stopped as Jesse turned around, pausing in his work.

"Ethan, hi!" Jesse called, setting his hammer down and coming over to give Ethan a bear hug.

"Hey, good to see you, man," Ethan said, slapping Jesse on the back.

"Is this the newly healed hand?" Jesse asked, stepping back to take a look at it.

"Still healing," Ethan replied, holding it up, "but it's practically good as new."

"Congratulations!" Jesse smiled broadly, his kindly eyes crinkling at the corners. "That's such good news."

"It's been a miracle," Sadie said, coming up behind them.

"Hey, babe," Ethan said, stepping to her and putting his arms around her. He smiled as she sank into his embrace. He had missed holding her like this. "It looks amazing in here! You all have gotten a lot done while I've been gone."

"I should have the rest of the kennels installed today," Jesse said, picking up his hammer again.

"And I was just finishing up in the office. I found a couple of desks at a liquidation sale for a really good deal, plus some office chairs," Sadie said.

"How about a grand tour?" Ethan asked.

"I thought you'd never ask," Sadie teased. "Come on, I'll show you around."

Ethan walked through the house with her, marveling at how fresh the paint looked, at the storage cabinets that had been set up to hold grooming supplies, dog food, and dog toys, and oohing and ahhing about how all of the minor details had come together to create a polished-looking kennel in general. He especially stopped to marvel at the grooming station Jesse had installed. It was spacious and perfect for grooming the dogs that would be boarded at the kennel. Ethan shook his head in wonder. He truly was amazed at his girlfriend's grit and tenacity to accomplish so much and he felt bad that he hadn't been able to help as much as he'd wanted to.

"Babe, it really looks amazing in here," he said as they returned to the front room. He pulled her into a hug again. "I can't believe the amount of work you've put into this! I mean, it's practically ready to open! Thank you so much for picking up the slack while I was in surgery. It means the world to me."

Sadie nodded, smiling a little, but her smile seemed suddenly brittle and she shrugged out of his embrace soon after. She ran a hand through her hair, looking away from him pointedly and pretending to watch Jesse work. Ethan cocked his head to the side, studying her. Something was off, but he wasn't sure what, or even why.

"Are you worried about opening the kennel?" he asked.

Sadie shook her head. "We can talk more about the kennel in the next few days. Right now what we need to focus on is the double wedding. I mean, it's almost here!" Her voice held a false note of cheer that was jarring to Ethan.

"But—" Ethan began to object. He wanted to know what was going on in the business, but before he could finish his sentence, Sadie's cell phone rang.

"I've got to take this," Sadie said quickly, stepping away and already putting the phone to her ear. She hurried out of the room.

Ethan stared after her, his brow furrowing as he watched the place where she had just been standing. Something was definitely off—she had shrugged off his talk about the business almost immediately, yet that was why he was at the kennel today in the first place. Why didn't she want to talk about it? Why was she evading his questions? And why did she seem so... different? Something was up, but he had no idea what it could be. He turned, noticing Jesse watching him.

"I'm not the only one who thought that was weird, right?" he said in a low voice to his friend. "Do you know what's going on with Sadie?"

Jesse sighed, setting his hammer down and taking a step closer to Ethan. He ran a hand through his hair, tousling it a little. "I've been talking to Addison, and apparently Sadie is really worried about the business."

"Why? Everything looks like it's going so well."

"It is," Jesse agreed, "but I think she's more

worried about the direction it will take in the future now that your hand has healed."

"I'm not following..."

"Sadie doesn't know if you plan to go back to being a vet now that your hand is better. And if you do, she's not sure what that will mean for the business." Jesse peered at him, clearly curious. "*Are* you planning to go back to being a vet?"

Ethan chewed the corner of his lip, thinking. "The thought had crossed my mind," he admitted.

Jesse nodded, folding his arms. "I can see why it would. Do you know what you're going to do?"

Ethan considered this, thinking hard. After a moment, the perfect idea occurred to him and a smile bloomed across his face. He could barely stand still. He was so excited. "I need to talk to Carolyn."

Jesse blinked, clearly not following. "Who's Carolyn?"

"She used to be my receptionist at the vet clinic."

"Why do you need to talk to her?"

Ethan's smile broadened and it was all he could do to resist literally rubbing his hands together in glee. "Because," he said. "I have an idea!"

CHAPTER TWENTY-ONE

Hector was just finishing up a showing for an adorable young couple looking to buy their first home when his cell phone buzzed in his pocket. He pulled it out to see Nadia's name on the screen. His heart leapt into his throat but he tried to maintain a calm presence for his clients. He slipped the phone back into his pocket, eager to get the couple on their way so that he could call Nadia back.

"I know this home didn't have the family room you were looking for, but it does have a great fenced-in backyard, which is unusual for a home this size," he said, leading the couple toward the front door.

"It's definitely something to think about!" the woman replied, leaning on her husband's arm. "We've got a lot to think about, but we'll give you a call soon either to move forward on this house or to keep looking."

"That sounds great," Hector said, reaching out to shake their hands, one after another. "Keep me posted."

"Will do," the man said, waving a goodbye and pulling the front door shut behind him.

Hector immediately snatched his phone from his pocket and pulled it out, eager to call Nadia back. She picked up on the second ring.

"Hello?"

"Hey, Nadia, it's me, sorry I missed your call."

"Oh, it's fine, no worries." There was a beat of silence, then Nadia continued, her voice a little shy. "I was wondering if you would come over to Addison and Jesse's house today."

Hector quickly went through his schedule in his mind, relieved that he had time to do as Nadia requested. "Sure thing. I can be over in about twenty minutes. Does that work?"

"Yup. Thanks," she replied. "I'll see you soon."

"Okay, bye."

Hector hung up, his heart racing. He hadn't heard much from Nadia since the bridal shower, when she had been so very, very distressed. He had hoped to be there for her in the aftermath of the disastrous meeting with her birth mother, but Nadia had said she wanted space, and Hector of course was not one to disrespect her wishes. He texted her every now and again to see how she was doing, but that had been the extent of their contact, so he was over the moon about the fact that she had called him and asked him to go see her.

Locking up the house behind him and whistling a jaunty tune, Hector hurried over to his car and climbed in, heading for Addison and Jesse's house. He thought of Nadia the entire drive, hoping that she was doing okay and thinking of her beautiful, dear face. The drive inched by for him, but finally he found himself pulling into Addison and Jesse's driveway. Once he had parked the car, he took a moment to take a deep breath and compose himself before heading up the front steps and knocking on the door.

Addison opened the door a moment later. "Hector, hello! So good to see you again!"

"Hi, Addison. Good to see you too."

"I assume you're here to see Nadia? Or is there some problem with Sadie and my property?"

Hector quickly shook his head, smiling up at her. "There's no problem with your property. You guessed it right the first time."

Addison smiled back, clearly relieved. "Well, come on in, then. Nadia's in the living room."

Hector followed Addison inside the house, glimpsing Nadia sitting on the floor playing with Lainey and Tyler. He paused for a moment, taking in the sight of her and admiring the way she made Lainey squeal with laughter as they played with Barbie dolls. She managed to do it all while holding Tyler in one arm too. Just then, Nadia looked up and saw Hector standing in the doorway. Her face broke into a huge smile, lighting up her eyes.

"Hector! Thanks for coming over," she said, climbing to her feet and handing the baby to Addison.

"Naddy! Play with me!" Lainey demanded.

"Nadia's busy right now," Addison told her, then turned to Nadia and Hector. "The house is a little crazy right now... maybe you two should take a walk?"

"Great idea," Nadia replied. "Is that okay with you, Hector?"

Hector nodded. "Sounds good to me."

A moment later he and Nadia headed out the front door, walking side by side down the quiet neighborhood sidewalk. Hector's heart was still thumping in his chest but he held his questions in, waiting for Nadia to speak first. A moment later, she did.

"I've missed seeing you," she said, her voice shy and quiet.

Hector's heart sped up even more. Tentatively, he took her hand, relieved when she didn't pull away. Instead, she threaded her fingers through his.

"I've missed you too."

"Sorry I've been MIA since the bridal shower," Nadia continued, glancing over at him. "I just needed some time by myself to process things."

"That's totally understandable. I think anyone in your shoes would've needed some time to come to terms with what happened. I mean, meeting your birth mother for the first time was a big deal."

"And it couldn't have gone worse," Nadia replied with a groan, rubbing her forehead with her free hand. She stopped walking and turned to face him. "All the same, thank you for being my date that day. It meant a lot to have your support."

Hector pulled her into a hug and she melted into his embrace. "I was happy to do it."

Hector held on for a moment longer, then released her, even though all he wanted to do was revel in the feel of her in his arms. They continued walking, neither speaking for a moment.

"I've been thinking," Nadia said after a short time. "I think I want to have a real conversation with Liz. One where I'm not just yelling at her, I mean."

"I think that's a great idea."

Nadia nodded. "I hope it is. I just think she deserves a chance to actually explain her side of the story without me attacking her." She paused. "I heard that Liz might be at the wedding, actually. I was thinking I could talk to her there." She pulled a face. "Of course, this time would be nothing like the bridal shower. I would keep my cool and not make a scene." Nadia sighed. "I can't believe I made such a ruckus at the bridal shower. I ruined it for everybody."

"Hey, slow down," Hector interjected. "No one that was there blames you for how you reacted, okay? You had a huge revelation sprung on you—no one would have handled that well."

"Thanks. That's sweet of you to say."

"I mean it," Hector insisted. "It was quite a shocking turn of events. So, are you still planning to go to the wedding knowing that she might be there?"

Nadia nodded. "I think so, yes. Actually, that's part of why I called you to come over today." Nadia looked shy again. "I was wondering if... you might want to be my date to the wedding? It's tomorrow, so I know it's short notice."

Hector beamed at her. "Of course! There's nothing I'd love more. I'll be your emotional support if things go awry with Liz."

Nadia squeezed his hand. "Thank you so much! You have no idea how much better I feel about the wedding knowing that you'll be with me." She paused again, a blush rising in her cheeks. "Actually, emotional support is not the reason I invited you. I want you to actually be my date... and I hope you'll be my date for more than just the wedding."

Hector's heart soared at her hinting words. "I'll be your date anytime, anywhere," he promised.

Nadia's smile widened and their eyes locked. Slowly, Hector lowered his mouth to hers and they shared the sweetest of kisses. After a moment they broke apart and Nadia's eyes fluttered open.

"You have no idea how long I've been wanting to do that," she whispered.

"Oh, yes I do," Hector countered with a laugh, "because I've been wanting to do that forever too."

* * *

Liz stared blankly at her laptop screen, trying to focus on work. She'd been sitting at the desk in her hotel room for hours, sending emails and taking phone calls, but her focus just wasn't in it, try as she might. That day she had been focusing on sending Charlotte's book to more publishers and she'd gotten a bite from a big one. It was exciting stuff, and she couldn't wait to tell Charlotte the news that she might soon have an official offer to present to her, but even with that amazing news Liz still couldn't focus. All she could think about was Nadia.

Everything about their first meeting had gone horribly wrong. It had been the exact opposite of how she had hoped things would turn out. In truth, she couldn't have pictured their first meeting going any worse than it had in reality. Liz scrubbed at her eyes, trying to erase the memories of Nadia's tearful, glaring eyes, of Nadia shouting at her, accusing her, of Nadia fleeing from the bistro. Liz shuddered, her eyes still covered as though that would help to make the memories go away. She had known that the first meeting was likely to be painful for many reasons, but she had never expected it to blow up so spectacularly.

And now, Liz thought, *there's no way she's ever*

going to want to talk to me again. I ruined my chance with her.

A knock at her hotel room door pulled her from her thoughts. Wearily, she rose from her desk chair and shuffled to the door, peering through the peephole. Seeing that Andy was standing on the other side, she pulled the door open, but she couldn't manage a smile for him.

"Hi, Andy," she said, her voice glum.

Andy took in her weary, red-rimmed eyes silently and then held up a paper bag. "I brought you some food. I figured you might not be eating as well as you should."

"I have been forgetting to eat," Liz admitted, letting him into the room.

"I thought so. Here, I brought some kugel and cholent—it's a stew with beans, potato, and brisket. It's hearty, feel-good food."

To her surprise, Liz found her stomach grumbling at the sight and scent of the food. She sat down at the little table across from Andy while he unpacked the containers. She hadn't eaten a decent meal since the bridal shower—mostly just snacking or having a light meal here and there, her appetite mostly gone. She'd lost a few pounds because of it and her face was looking more gaunt when she looked in the bathroom mirror. But now, with Andy's reassuring presence, she found that she was ready to eat a real meal for the first time in many days.

Liz spooned up a bite and groaned softly, savoring the hearty flavors. She quickly took another bite. "Thank you so much. This is just what I needed."

"I'm glad you like it," Andy said, taking a bite of the kugel. He peered at her, studying her face. "How have you been doing?" he asked, his voice gentle.

Liz shrugged, not meeting his eyes. "I'm fine."

"No, you're not. Come on, talk to me."

Liz finally met his gaze and the tenderness in his eyes nearly undid her. "I can't stop thinking about Nadia," she admitted. "I need to find a way to reconcile with her. I can't let things go on as they have been."

Andy nodded slowly. "Won't she be at the wedding tomorrow? Maybe that would be a good time to talk to her."

Liz shook her head. "I wouldn't dream of causing another scene on Elise's and Charlotte's special day. What if Nadia is still angry?"

"I don't know... she's had time to cool off and come to terms with everything. I bet she knows you've been invited, so she's probably already planning on the fact that you'll be there."

"Do you really think so?"

"I do," Andy said firmly. "I think the wedding could be the perfect place to have a healing moment with your daughter."

Liz took another bite of stew, mulling his words over. "I just don't want to ruin the wedding like I ruined the bridal shower."

"You won't," Andy insisted. "If it looks like it might head that way, you and I can leave. How does that sound?"

Liz chewed on the corner of her lip, thinking hard. She desperately wanted to see Nadia again and Andy might be right— the wedding might be the perfect place to have a healing conversation with her daughter.

"Okay," she said softly. "I'll go."

CHAPTER TWENTY-TWO

Though her heart soared with such excitement that she felt almost jittery, Charlotte's hands were steady as she unzipped her simple sheath wedding dress and stepped into it, zipping up the back behind herself. She gazed into the mirror, pleased at how she looked in her simple yet elegant dress. Most of all, though, she noticed the way she practically seemed to glow—joy radiated from her eyes, from the upturned curve of her lips, almost from her very skin.

"Today is the day," she whispered to her reflection, brushing her long, loose curls out of her face. "Today is the day I marry the love of my life."

Even speaking the words it still didn't feel true. She almost wondered if she should pinch herself— she couldn't believe that after so much waiting and planning she was going to marry the handsomest, kindest, most loving man in the world. Briggs might not look like much to others, but for Charlotte he was everything. A knock at the front door pulled her from her contemplations and she checked the clock on the wall, which told her it must be her sister and her mother.

"Come in!" she called at the top of the stairs.

The front door opened and Nina and Melissa stepped inside, both coming to a halt in the foyer to stare up at her. Even Melissa was speechless for a moment as she gazed up at her daughter. Soon, though, both mother and daughter were hurrying up the stairs to get a closer look at Charlotte.

"Your dress is stunning on you," Nina said, pulling her sister into a hug, careful not to wrinkle the dress. "It's so simple that it makes you shine all the more."

"Thank you!"

Melissa, however, was viewing her daughter with a critical eye. "Why didn't you pick something with a little more embellishment? Some lace or beading never hurt anybody." She tutted. "Oh, and your hair! Charlotte, it's too simple in loose curls like that. You need to pull it up into a formal updo."

Charlotte inhaled deeply, feeling her nostrils

flaring. She had endured much of her mother's criticism over the years, but today she was finished with it. She had kept silent while her mother had been visiting Sea Breeze Cove, even when her mother made disparaging remarks about Briggs's profession and the simplicity of the wedding shower, but no more.

"Mom," she said, her voice firm. "I know what you're saying is coming from a place of love, but the judgment and criticism has to stop. It doesn't help anything."

Melissa blinked, stunned and clearly in shock, even though Charlotte's words had been much milder than what she wanted to say.

"Rather than focus on all the external details," Charlotte continued, "I think the most important thing is whether Nina and I are happy." She looked at her sister, who was nodding. "And I would say we both are."

"Yes," Nina added quickly. "We are."

Charlotte smoothed the front of her dress, trying not to squirm in the silence that followed. It had taken a lot for her to finally speak up about her feelings to her mother, and she hoped she hadn't caused irreparable damage there. If Melissa took things the wrong way, she might have, but it had still needed to be said. Melissa's face crumbled a little and she looked downcast, chagrined even.

"I'm so sorry," Melissa said, her voice low. "I had no idea my comments were so hurtful. I mean," she fluttered her hands in front of herself, "I was just trying to be helpful and look out for my daughters. I only want the best for both of you, but... but I suppose I must have come off as overbearing."

Charlotte's guarded expression softened at her mother's simple words. She stepped over to Melissa and pulled her into a hug, feeling Nina join them a moment later. They all stayed that way for a minute, mother and daughters tangled together in a loving embrace, before Charlotte finally stepped back and looked at her mother.

"Thank you for what you said. I know what I told you wasn't easy to hear."

"It wasn't," Melissa admitted, "but I'm proud of you for saying it all the same. I'll try to be less critical. But do know that I won't be perfect at first—please, be patient with me."

"You know that we will," Nina said, reaching out to squeeze her mother's hand.

Melissa sighed, giving both of them a watery

smile. "You know, I've been thinking I might want to move to Sea Breeze Cove. I miss living near my daughters and I want to live closer to you."

"Wow," Charlotte said, utterly surprised. "That's a big change..."

"I know, but sometimes that's what it takes." Melissa checked her watch. "My goodness, look at the time! I'll let you two have a moment together, but I'm going to go claim my seat at the beach."

"Okay, Mom," Nina said. "I'll be there in a few minutes."

Melissa kissed Charlotte's cheek and then patted it. "I'm happy for you, my dear."

Charlotte felt tears rising in her eyes. "Thanks, Mom," she whispered.

Melissa nodded and then turned and walked back down the stairs, exiting quietly through the front door. Nina turned and looked at her sister with wide, astonished eyes.

"I can't believe she's thinking of moving here!" she blurted out.

"It could be a good thing," Charlotte replied. "She took what I said well and she said she's going to work on it, so maybe it won't be like before."

"I think you're right," Nina agreed, her

expression becoming thoughtful. "I mean, I know she's not going to change overnight, or even change completely, but at least now she knows that her judgmental comments just drive a wedge between her and us."

"Any effort she makes to be less judgmental will be greatly appreciated. I'm honestly happy at the thought that she wants to live closer to us."

"I'm surprised to say it, but I am too." Nina looked at Charlotte, a wide smile returning to her face. "Oh, Char, I'm so happy for you! I can't believe you're getting married today!"

"I know, I can barely believe it myself!"

"But it's happening, and you look absolutely gorgeous."

"Thanks, sis," Charlotte said, tucking a strand of hair behind her ear. "I'm glad you're doing so well in life too. Oliver is a gem."

"That he is." Nina hugged her arms to herself, smiling. "And to think, all of this happened because you made the decision to move to Sea Breeze Cove! I thought you were crazy at the time, but look at all the good things that have come from it. It's truly a magical place."

Charlotte grinned. "I can't dispute you on that."

Nina pulled her phone from her tiny handbag and gasped. "Look at the time! Come on, we'd better head over to the beach. You can't be late to your own wedding!"

Elise looked around at the elegant setup on the beach. People had called them crazy for planning a beach wedding instead of booking a venue, but she and Charlotte had been firm. They wanted to be married out of doors and beside the ocean. Everything was looking perfect—rows of white wooden chairs faced a flowered arch, wide enough for both couples to stand. Vases of the same flowers flanked each row of chairs, forming a long, flowered aisle for Elise and Charlotte to walk down.

Even though everything looked perfect, Elise was still feeling jittery as she gazed at the rows of seats filling up with guests. Weddings were such a big deal, even simple affairs like this one, and there was so much pressure to make sure it all went perfectly. What if something happened, like a sudden rainstorm or another altercation like what had occurred at the wedding shower? What if she tripped walking down the aisle and tore her dress?

Or worse, what if Gabe got cold feet and left Elise standing alone at the proverbial altar?

That last worry Elise managed to shake off. She knew Gabe would never do that to her. If anything, *she* was the one with wedding jitters, not him. Still, even with that worry cast aside, a ball of nerves still squirmed in her belly and she thought she might be sick. Bridget, who was serving as her maid of honor, showed up a moment later, coming to stand beside Elise. She looked up at her friend's face, seeming to see the wedding jitters seething within Elise.

"I have to tell you something," Bridget said.

"What? What is it?" Elise demanded, already imagining the worst.

"Calm down, it's good," Bridget assured her. "I was just with the two grooms and I heard them talking and do you want to know what Gabe said?"

Elise nodded eagerly, her nerves still squirming within.

"He said that he knew you were nervous about today and that he was willing to forego the whole wedding entirely if that's what would make you happy. He said all he wants is to be with you and he doesn't care whether the two of you get married today or ten years from today. All he wants is you."

Elise felt tears rising in her eyes even as the

nausea-inducing knot in her stomach relaxed. "He said that?"

Bridget nodded. "I wasn't supposed to hear, but I'm glad I did."

Elise reached out and squeezed Bridget's hand. "I'm glad you heard it too."

And it was true. Knowing that Gabe just wanted to be with her and that he was willing to wait for marriage if that was what she wanted just made her all the more certain that now was the right time to get married. They weren't doing it for the wrong reasons—to keep up with friends or impress anyone. No, they already knew that they wanted to be together for the long haul, wedding or no wedding. In fact, she knew that Gabe would marry her in a courthouse privately if that was what she wanted, and the knowledge of his love and steadiness steadied her. She took in a few deep breaths, feeling worlds better than she had been just a minute before.

"He's the right one for you," Bridget said softly. "Lean into that love you have for him. I did that when it came to Timothy and it's been amazing what that trust has done for us."

"You're right," Elise said simply. "You turned your life around and found happiness. If you can do it, I'm going to rise to the challenge and do it too."

"That's the spirit!" Bridget said, pulling her friend into a hug. "I'm so happy for you," she whispered before pulling back. "Today is going to be a wonderful day."

"I'm beginning to think you're right," Elise agreed, squeezing Bridget's hand.

"Is that my little girl?" Arthur asked, coming up behind them. His eyes sparkled with tears as he looked down at his daughter. "I can't believe my little girl is getting married today. I'm so proud of you, sweetheart. Gabe is a good man."

Elise threw her arms around her father, pulling him close. Even just a few months ago he wouldn't have said those words, and hearing them now meant everything to her. Her father hugged her back tightly, and Elise felt even more calm as she hugged him. Today *was* going to be a good day. She just needed to have the courage not to let her worries get the best of her.

"Are you ready to walk down the aisle?" Arthur whispered, pulling back from the hug and searching his daughter's eyes.

Elise nodded. "Yes, I finally am."

"That's my girl." Arthur tucked Elise's hand into the crook of his arm and patted it. "After you, Bridget."

The music began playing and Bridget, with one last glowing look at Elise, led the way down the aisle, Elise and Arthur close behind.

CHAPTER TWENTY-THREE

As the officiant spoke words about the sanctity of marriage as a union of love, Charlotte gazed around her. Nina stood by her side as her maid of honor and Jesse, Briggs's best man, stood at Briggs's side. On the other side of the arch, Bridget stood at Elise's side as maid of honor and Ethan stood beside Gabe as best man. Charlotte sighed happily, so grateful to see so many happy and smiling faces looking up at them from the rows of white chairs. Today was going beautifully, down to the perfect weather surrounding them.

Briggs caught Charlotte's wandering gaze and he raised one eyebrow in question but she merely smiled radiantly at him. Of all the wonderful people there to support the two couples, the most important person of all was Briggs. She couldn't believe that it was finally happening, that she was finally being joined in matrimony to the love of her life.

"And now, it's time for the vows," the officiant was saying. "It's my understanding that each couple wrote their own vows."

The two couples nodded.

"Charlotte and Briggs, we'll begin with you. Charlotte?"

Charlotte nodded, taking the microphone and turning to look deeply into Briggs's eyes. "Briggs, I've thought a lot about what I wanted to say to you today, and everything I wrote kept falling short. How do you tell the love of your life what he means to you? Where are the words?"

Briggs's eyes were already beginning to mist over with tears and he reached out to hold her hand, squeezing it softly. Charlotte smiled at him apologetically.

"I'm afraid all I have are wholly inadequate words to tell you that I love you. Forever. Who would have thought that moving to Sea Breeze Cove and having my car spin out would lead me to the man of my dreams? Briggs, you are everything to me. Everything. And I plan to spend the rest of our lives trying to make you as happy as you make me. This is my promise to you."

Charlotte handed the microphone over to Briggs, who had to take a moment to clear his throat and wipe at his eyes. A few members of the audience were wiping at their eyes as well, and Charlotte could already feel tears rising in her own eyes.

"Charlotte, my love," Briggs said, his voice husky with emotion. "You did the impossible. You brought healing to my broken heart. I thought the kind of heartbreak I experienced when I lost my first wife and son was something I would never, ever be able to recover from. I thought happiness and love were over for me, that life was merely about getting through each day. And then you came into my life, so unexpectedly, and turned my entire world upside down. Charlotte, you are my whole world now, and I want to spend the rest of my life showing you the kind of love you show me every day. I promise that no matter what happens, rain or shine, I will be by your side, loving you more and more every day."

Charlotte dabbed at her eyes, smiling at her soon-to-be husband. His words were simple too, and utterly perfect. Briggs handed the microphone to Elise, who stood waiting. Elise took the microphone and turned to face Gabe.

"Gabe, you've been a part of my life for as long as I can remember. Who would've thought that us two childhood best friends would end up getting married one day? You've been my friend for so long, and now my love for a short time. I wish I could go back in time and date you sooner," she said, and the crowd chuckled appreciatively. Elise laughed as well, then sobered. "It hasn't been an easy road getting here, but it's been so worth it. I wouldn't trade any of our time together for the world. Gabe, you are the love of my life, the reason I'm standing here today ready to pledge my commitment to you in front of our family and friends. I love you, and I'm going to keep loving you, every day that we have together as long as we both shall live and beyond."

Elise handed the microphone to Gabe who was by now misty-eyed.

"How can I follow that?" he asked, and the crowd laughed. Gabe became serious then. "Elise, I thought I missed my chance at happiness a long time ago. I thought I had made too many mistakes to ever find love again, but you showed me how wrong I was. You saved me, and I'm going to spend the rest of my life trying to show you how much that means to me." He cleared his throat, dabbing at his eyes. "I don't have adequate words to tell you what you mean to me, but rest assured that I will spend the rest of our lives trying to find enough ways to tell you and show you that you are my entire world, my entire life. Elise, I love you now and I will love you forever."

Gabe handed the microphone to the officiant, who took it. "I understand that the two couples want to say their 'I do's' at the same time?"

Charlotte, Briggs, Elise, and Gabe all nodded. "We do," they said, and the crowd laughed again.

"In that case, Charlotte and Elise—Charlotte, do you take Briggs to be your lawfully wedded husband, and, Elise, do you take Gabe to be your lawfully wedded husband?"

"I do," Charlotte and Elise chorused.

"And, Briggs, do you take Charlotte to be your lawfully wedded wife? Gabe, do you take Elise to be your lawfully wedded wife?"

"I do," Briggs and Gabe said at the same time.

"In that case, I now pronounce you man and wife," he said to Charlotte and Briggs, "and man and wife," he said to Gabe and Elise. "Husbands, you may now kiss your brides."

At the same time, Briggs gathered Charlotte into his arms and Gabe leaned down to kiss and embrace Elise, his new wife. Charlotte melted into Briggs's embrace, kissing him back wholeheartedly as the crowd whooped and hollered, clapping their hearts out in celebration of the newly minted husbands and wives. Charlotte reveled in the moment, knowing that she would remember this moment for the rest of her life.

Nadia followed the rest of the guests to Brady's Bar, just a few blocks into downtown, where the two happy couples had planned an informal and somewhat intimate reception. Hector held her hand as they walked.

"Wasn't that a beautiful ceremony?" she asked, tucking her dark hair behind her ear as a light breeze caught at it.

"It was perfect," Hector agreed. "Don't tell anyone I told you this, but I'm a sucker for weddings. I cry every time."

"You big softie," Nadia teased, ribbing him lightly with her elbow.

"What can I say? My mother raised me on a lot of Hallmark movies," he joked, making Nadia laugh. Hector held open the door of Brady's Bar. "After you."

Nadia thanked him and then stepped inside,

pausing to admire the twinkle lights festooned across the ceiling of the bar and the flowers on the wooden bar countertop. It was very simply decorated, but it was perfect to her. She glanced over at Charlotte, Briggs, Elise, and Gabe who were surrounded by a crowd of well-wishers and saw from the radiant, glowing smiles on their faces that the reception was everything they had hoped it would be too.

Hector and Nadia got in line to wish the happy couples well. Finally, after waiting for a few minutes, it was their turn.

"Congratulations!" Nadia said, pulling Charlotte and then Elise into a hug. "I'm so happy for all of you!"

"Thank you," Charlotte said, squeezing Nadia's hand. "I'm so glad you came today."

"Me too."

Hector was shaking hands with first Briggs, then Gabe. "Congratulations, you two. Beautiful ceremony."

"Thanks so much," Gabe responded. "Enjoy yourself now, okay? There's some really good food lined up. I just hope there's some left when we're finished with the receiving line," he joked.

"I'll enjoy it for you," Hector joked back.

Hector, putting his hand on the small of Nadia's

back, guided her past the couples and toward an empty table. "Want me to get you some food?"

"That would be great," Nadia agreed.

True to his word, Hector returned a few minutes later with two plates loaded down with bruschetta with sauteed radishes and marinated olives, and a flatbread lined with cheddar, pancetta, and apple. Nadia's stomach growled hungrily at the sight of the food and she rubbed her hands together playfully, making Hector laugh.

Before she dug in, however, Nadia found herself studying Hector's handsome face.

"What is it?" he asked around a mouthful of flatbread. "Do I have something on my face?"

Nadia laughed. "Not at all. I was just thinking how nice this is. Thank you for being my date."

Hector swallowed his bite and grinned. "I will happily assume that role for the foreseeable future. As long as you'll let me."

Nadia leaned forward and so did Hector, their lips meeting in a tender kiss.

"Well," Nadia whispered, "get ready, because I'm not planning to let you go anytime soon."

Hector pressed another kiss to her lips before sitting back. "I wouldn't have it any other way," he said with a wink that made Nadia's heart flutter.

Nadia was just taking a bite of the bruschetta when she felt someone's eyes on her. She turned in her seat and saw Liz watching her from across the room. Nadia's stomach lurched and her heart began to race. She swallowed her bite, nearly choking on it. She had tried to focus on the ceremony and the happy couples all day, but now she could no longer ignore the fact that her birth mother was also in attendance.

Would she have the courage to approach Liz before the night was out? Nadia took in a shuddering breath, her palms sweating a little. Would Liz even want to talk to her after the way Nadia had treated her at the wedding shower? Was she even ready to have another conversation?

CHAPTER TWENTY-FOUR

Sadie smiled at Charlotte and Elise, pulling one after another into a hug. "You both made such beautiful brides," she said when she stepped back and took in their dresses all over again. "Today has been perfect."

"It has," Elise admitted. "And to think, I almost didn't walk down the aisle at all."

"Really?"

"Really," Elise confirmed, pulling Bridget, who was standing beside her, into a quick hug. "You can thank this amazing woman right here for giving me the courage to make the best decision of my life."

"Oh, hush," Bridget said with a laugh. "You already had the courage, I just gave you a little nudge in the right direction."

Just then, the strains of music for the first dance

struck up over the bar's speakers and Charlotte and Elise looked at each other.

"That's our cue," Charlotte said. "Elise?"

Elise nodded and the two brides went to find their husbands for the first dance. Sadie took a sip of champagne, watching them as Briggs led Charlotte to the makeshift dance floor in the middle of the bar and Gabe and Elise began slow dancing together. She sighed happily for her friends, content that all had gone beautifully today.

There's really nothing that could make this day better, she thought, taking another sip of champagne and smiling as Briggs twirled Charlotte and then dipped her.

"Hey, sweetheart," a voice whispered in her ear.

Sadie didn't even jump, although she hadn't heard Ethan approach. She smiled up at him, leaning back against his chest as his arms encircled her waist. They watched the dancers for a moment in silence, then Ethan whispered in her ear.

"Can we talk for a minute?"

"Hmm?" It took Sadie a moment to process what he had said, consumed as she was in watching Charlotte and Elise dancing with their new husbands.

"Can we talk for a minute?"

Sadie turned around in his arms, looking up at him. His eyes were excited, but his expression was serious. Sadie suddenly felt a chill run through her and she knew this was it—this was the moment that Ethan was going to tell her that he could no longer run the business alongside her. She braced herself, taking a deep breath in an attempt to soothe the nerves that had suddenly enveloped her.

"Sadie, I—"

Suddenly she couldn't bear it. She cut him off. "Ethan, let me talk first. I already know what you're going to say."

Ethan's brow furrowed. "You do?"

Sadie nodded. "I've thought things through—trust me, I've done a *lot* of thinking. And I want you to know, I'm truly so overjoyed about your hand, that you were able to get the surgery and that it has healed and given you your life back." She took another deep breath, realizing that she wasn't sounding very coherent. "What I'm trying to say is, I understand completely if you've decided you want to go back to being a veterinarian."

Sadie bit her lip to physically stop herself from babbling even more. She had said what she needed to say and now it was her turn to listen to Ethan and gracefully accept the news she was sure he was going to give her. But, as Ethan opened his mouth to speak, she found that she still didn't have the courage to hear him. At least not yet.

"And," she continued hastily, "Addison and I will find a way to make things work without you. We'll be fine. And, you know, maybe when you have a minute here or there in your schedule as a vet you can still help us out when you can. I mean, that would be so helpful and—"

But here Ethan cut her off by pulling her into his arms and planting a kiss on her still-moving lips. Only when the kiss deepened did she stop trying to talk and surrender to his embrace.

"There," he whispered, pulling back. "That's better. Are you going to let me talk now?"

"Mmhmm," Sadie murmured, nodding meekly.

Ethan cupped Sadie's face in his hands, staring deeply into her eyes. "I have something to tell you."

Sadie shuddered. "So just tell me. I'm dying over here."

Ethan chuckled, his eyes crinkling at the corners. "Well, I've been trying to, you know."

Sadie pulled a face but didn't say anything, vowing this time to stay silent so that he could actually speak.

Ethan took a deep breath. "I've been talking to Carolyn."

Sadie's heart sank in spite of herself. So he *was* going to reopen his veterinarian practice.

"And she said she was willing to come back and work for me... at the kennel."

It took Sadie a moment to register his words. "...at the kennel?"

Ethan nodded, smiling. "At the kennel," he confirmed. "The best blessing of my hand healing is that I get to do more for *our* business. Together, we can corner the market as a one-stop shop for all the needs of Sea Breeze Cove's pets. We can groom them, board them, give them vet check-ups, and walk them. They won't need to go anywhere else."

Sadie stared up at him, utterly speechless. She had no words as she struggled to process what he had just said.

"I'm sorry I didn't tell you sooner," Ethan continued, caressing her cheek with his thumb. "I had to check with Carolyn first to make sure that she was on board." His brow creased and he searched her eyes. "I had hoped you'd be delighted with the surprise..." His face fell as he took in her still-silent countenance. "I'm sorry if my attempt to surprise you caused you any distress, I—"

But now it was Sadie's turn to cut him off with a sweet kiss. When she finally pulled back, she was smiling. "Don't you dare apologize," she whispered fiercely. "You've given me the best gift! I was so sad when I thought I had lost you as a business partner, because I love working with you. You've made it so you can still be a vet *and* build a business with me. It's the perfect plan."

Ethan lowered his head and kissed her fervently. "I'm just so excited to continue building a life with you, my love."

Sadie rested in his embrace for another long moment before a thought occurred to her. She lifted her head and looked up at Ethan excitedly. "Come on, we need to tell Addison and Jesse! This concerns them too!"

"You're very right," Ethan agreed. "Lead the way."

Sadie grabbed Ethan's hand and wove through the crowd of friends and family to find Addison and Jesse standing at the edge of the dance floor, watching the couples dancing. Sadie waved to get their attention and then pulled them off to the side.

"You two," Sadie said breathlessly when Addison and Jesse turned to her and Ethan. "I have the best news! Ethan just told me that he's bringing his former receptionist, Carolyn, on board and that he wants to add his vet practice to our business!"

"That's brilliant!" Addison breathed. "That way, pets in Sea Breeze Cove won't have to go anywhere else—they'll come to us for everything!"

"That's exactly the idea," Ethan chimed in, beaming.

"Awesome idea, man," Jesse said, reaching out to shake Ethan's hand. "I can't believe we all didn't think of it sooner."

As the group excitedly talked of future plans for the business moving forward, Sadie hugged Ethan close. All of her hopes and dreams for the future were fully restored and healed, just as Ethan's hand had been fully restored and healed.

Nadia stared at her empty plate. She had vowed to herself that when she had finished eating the food Hector had brought her that she would go and talk to Liz. Well, now the plate was finished but she still hadn't found the courage to actually follow through on her silent goal. As if reading her mind, Hector leaned over and squeezed her hand.

"I can walk with you if you want," he said in a low voice.

Nadia blinked. "Was I that obvious?"

Hector nodded with a smile. "I know you've been wanting to talk to Liz for a while now. I just figured you were trying to work up the courage."

"You can read me like a book," Nadia sighed. "But yes, I would love it if you walked over with me. I think that would help."

Hector stood and held out his hand to Nadia. After debating within herself for another silent moment, she finally stood and took his hand. Hector squeezed it, smiling at her reassuringly. Together, they wove through the crowd until they got to the table in the corner where Liz sat with Andy. Upon seeing them approach, Andy scooted closer to Liz, putting his arm around her and watching Nadia carefully, as if waiting to see if she was going to explode and cause a scene. Nadia caught Hector signaling Andy to back off and, a moment later, Andy whispered something in Liz's ear and melted into the crowd. At the same time, Hector squeezed Nadia's hand one last time and then stepped away, leaving just Liz and Nadia alone.

Nadia stood frozen for a moment, but then she cleared her throat. "May I sit?"

Liz nodded mutely, simply watching Nadia carefully. Nadia sat down and finally looked at her birth mother—really looked. Her eyes roved over Liz's face as she searched for, and found, bits of her own face in her birth mother's face.

Liz sighed, breaking the silence. "I need you to believe that I really wanted to keep you," she said, her voice strained and low. "I wanted to try and raise you all by myself, but I also knew that I couldn't give you what a stable, happy family could. I wanted you to be well-cared for."

Nadia gave Liz a shy half-smile. "I *was* well-loved by my adoptive parents, so you were right about that."

Liz smiled, looking relieved. The tightness around her eyes eased somewhat as she listened to Nadia.

Nadia took a deep breath. "I can understand why you gave me away, but why did you take so long to seek me out? I mean, you've been in Sea Breeze Cove for ages. Why wait so long?"

Liz twisted her hands in her lap. "Because I was afraid," she said softly.

"Afraid? Of what?"

Liz finally met Nadia's gaze. "Of you. Of how

you would perceive the mistakes I made in the past. I wasn't sure you would even want to get to know me."

Nadia nodded slowly. "I suppose I can understand that," she admitted.

"But we're both here now," Liz continued. "We've found each other again, and maybe it's a chance for us to get to know one another better."

Nadia chewed the corner of her lip for a few seconds, debating internally. Was she ready for that? On the other hand, wasn't finding her birth mother what she had wanted for ages?

"You might be right," Nadia finally said. She hesitated. "Are... are you planning to stay in Sea Breeze Cove?"

"I've already been splitting my time between New York City and Sea Breeze Cove, and I plan to keep doing that. I might even stay here full-time and just head back to New York for really important business meetings I can't miss." Liz smiled. "I love it here. You're here. And there's a man here I'm starting to have feelings for."

Nadia nodded. "This town is a special place. It's a good place to heal. I've found happiness working for Addison and things are moving forward with Hector. If you'd asked me if I would be okay six months ago, I wouldn't have thought so, but, like I said—there's just something about this town."

"I'm beginning to see that." Liz looked excited. "If we both stay in Sea Breeze Cove, does that mean there's a chance for us to get to know each other better?"

Nadia smiled at her birth mother, this time a real and full smile, not something small and shy. "I like the sound of your plan."

"Excellent!" Liz looked pleased and relieved. "Let's start right now. You're in college, right? Tell me about your classes."

Nadia launched into a description of her university courses and Liz reminisced about her own college days. They had been talking for a good ten minutes or so, really relaxing and enjoying one another's company, when Liz's cell phone rang. Liz looked down at the screen and then jumped to her feet.

"This is an important call," she said. "I've got to take this, I'm so sorry!"

"It's fine," Nadia said, waving her away with a smile. "We've got plenty of time to catch up."

Liz grinned, then pressed the phone to her ear as she stepped away. Nadia sat back in her seat, marveling at the change the last few minutes had brought into her life. Her heart, which had been so torn and full of nerves for so long, finally felt settled in her chest. Life was looking up for her—things with her adoptive parents were getting better and now she was beginning to forge a new relationship with her birth mother.

Addison was right, she thought. *Family can mean whatever you want it to mean, and mine is large.*

Nadia looked around the crowded room full of family and friends that loved her. Yes, family could mean whatever one wanted it to mean, and she had found hers. She rose to find Hector so they could dance, thinking all the while that, at that moment, she felt like the luckiest girl in the world.

CHAPTER TWENTY-FIVE

Charlotte wrapped her arms more closely around Briggs's neck, pulling him closer as they swayed on the dance floor. The lights strung up across the bar twinkled above them, making the moment feel magical and ethereal.

"I'm so happy," she whispered, closing her eyes as she tucked her face into Briggs's neck. "I feel like I could fly over the moon."

"Me too," Briggs murmured, his breath warm on her ear, ruffling her hair a little.

Charlotte pulled back a little to look him in the eye. "And today went perfectly, don't you think?"

Briggs nodded. "All that planning paid off. And the weather was perfect too."

"To be honest, I still would've thought it was a

perfect day even if the sky opened and rained buckets on us while we were saying our vows. All that matters is that now I'm your wife and you're my husband."

"I couldn't agree more," Briggs whispered, kissing her first on her nose, then her cheeks, then finally pressing a sweet kiss to her lips.

Charlotte leaned into his kiss, still swaying, and basked in the perfect happiness of the moment. And to think, just a few months ago, she was struggling with whether she should accept Briggs's proposal or not! The thought seemed absurd now, and she knew with all her heart and down to her very bones that she had just made the best decision of her life.

"By the way," Briggs said, whispering in her ear again. "I have a surprise for you."

"A surprise?" Charlotte pulled back to look into his eyes, searching them even as a smile grew on her face. "What is it?"

Briggs pulled her closer to him again and grinned roguishly as he looked into her eyes. "You'll need to pack up a bag tonight."

Charlotte raised her eyebrows in question. "Ooh, why?"

"Well, I took care of our honeymoon, just like I promised I would. We're heading out for a sun-splashed getaway—I have two tickets for us to head to Aruba in the morning."

Charlotte bit back a squeal of delight, her smile spreading across her face. "Are you serious? Don't mess with me, love."

"I'm dead serious. There's a resort in Aruba with our names on it."

Charlotte did a little happy dance, making Briggs laugh. "I can't wait! How did you know?"

"I know you," Briggs replied with a laugh, kissing her on her nose again. "And don't worry about Bruno —I already talked to Sadie and Ethan and Bruno is going to be the very first resident of their kennel."

"You've thought of everything!"

"I told you I would."

"Thank you so much," Charlotte murmured, nuzzling closer to him. Happiness spread through her, like sunshine lighting up her veins. "I can't wait to snuggle with you on the white sands of Aruba." Charlotte looked up at him, her eyes suddenly misty. "You know, getting my car stuck in the sand that one day was the best thing that ever happened to me."

"And helping the cute girl having car trouble was the best thing that ever happened to *me,*" Briggs agreed. He leaned down, and their lips met in a tender kiss. Briggs pulled her closer, his arms around her waist.

As they broke apart, Charlotte saw movement out of the corner of her eye. She turned her head to see Liz hurrying toward them, looking very excited.

"Charlotte!" Liz called, stopping next to them, a little breathless. "I'm so sorry to interrupt."

"No, it's fine. What's up?"

Liz took a deep breath, her smile growing. "I know I shouldn't be talking business on your wedding day, but I thought you'd want to hear this."

Charlotte waited on tenterhooks.

"I just got off the phone with a major publisher, and they made a formal offer for your book!"

Charlotte felt her jaw drop. "Are you serious? Please tell me you're serious."

"I'm serious," Liz said with a laugh. "You're going to be a published author!"

Charlotte squealed and threw her arms around Liz, not caring that it wasn't professional. "Thank you so much for making this happen! I can't believe it!"

"Believe it," Liz replied with a sassy grin. "Your name is going to be on the cover of your very own published book."

Charlotte shook her head, still in disbelief. "Thank you for telling me."

"I thought you'd want to hear right away." Liz took a step back. "This is the start of something wonderful for you, I can feel it. And I look forward to working with you on many other future books."

"Me too," Charlotte agreed, still a bit dazed. "Thank you so much."

"Of course. Well, I'll let you get back to dancing," Liz said with a wave and hurried off the dance floor.

Charlotte turned back to Briggs, her eyes wide.

"This day just got even more perfect," he said, grinning down at her. "I'm so proud of you."

"Thank you," she whispered, snuggling close to him. "I can't believe one person can experience this much happiness!"

"Well, you better believe it, because I plan on keeping you this happy for the rest of our lives."

* * *

Elise had managed to snag a piece of wedding cake before it was all gone, but folks still kept coming up to her and Gabe to wish them well, so she had to sneak bites in between visits from guests. She was starting to get very tired, although she was feeling awash with contentment that the day had gone off beautifully. Gabe caught her eye and gave her a mischievous look.

"Want to sneak out of here for a breath of fresh air?" he murmured in her ear.

Elise nodded quickly. "I would love to."

"Come on," he whispered, taking her hand. "Let's make a break for it before someone else stops us!"

Hand in hand, Elise and Gabe snuck out the front door of Brady's Bar and began walking down the sidewalk until they found a quiet alcove next to the side of one business. Gabe took Elise by the waist, making her laugh, and pulled her into the alcove, where he kissed her long and deeply.

"I've been wanting to do that all day," he said when they broke apart.

Elise blinked, a little dazed from his kiss. "Me too," she murmured back, feeling like she'd just drunk a glass of wine. Gabe still had that effect on her.

Gabe looked down at her and squeezed her hand, suddenly looking sheepish.

Elise raised her eyebrows. "What's wrong?"

Gabe twisted his lips to the side. "Well... I

overheard Briggs telling Charlotte about some surprise tickets he booked for their honeymoon tomorrow morning. They're going to Aruba."

"Good for them! Why is that a problem?"

"It's not a problem, it's just that... well... I kind of feel like now the honeymoon I planned for you isn't good enough."

Elise put a hand on his arm, squeezing it gently. "I'm sure that isn't true, love. What is it?"

Gabe looked reluctant, biting his lip.

"Come on, Gabe. You can tell me. After all, I'm your wife now—no secrets between us!"

Gabe laughed. "I can't argue with that." He took a deep breath, his words coming out in a rush. "I just... after so much time being just friends with you, I wanted to celebrate being married to you right here in Sea Breeze Cove. I booked us a few different bed and breakfasts in and around Sea Breeze Cove so that we can revisit some of our favorite places as husband and wife. I thought it would be cool to re-experience this town as a married couple." Gabe's face fell. "Now I know that probably wasn't such a cool idea. It sounded better in my head." He sighed. "I've been saving up for a big honeymoon trip, so we can do something grander if you'd prefer."

"Oh, Gabe," Elise said, throwing her arms

around his neck and pulling him close. "What did I ever do to deserve you?"

Gabe wrapped his arms around her waist and when he chuckled she could feel it vibrating through her body. "It's the opposite, love. What did *I* do to deserve you?"

"As for the honeymoon," Elise said, pausing to kiss him softly, "I love your idea! We can do a big trip later on—maybe for our one year anniversary. For now, I'm over the moon to do your staycation honeymoon and spend time together in the place where we fell in love."

"Are you sure?"

Elise nodded, kissing him again to put his mind at ease. "I couldn't be more sure. It's a beautiful idea and I can't wait to experience Sea Breeze Cove not as your friend or your girlfriend, but as your wife."

A grin split Gabe's face and he looked relieved and pleased that she liked the idea. Elise snuggled closer into his arms.

"Oh, my love," she murmured, releasing a sigh of happiness. "I'm so grateful that you and I took the leap from friendship to more."

"Me too," he agreed, kissing the top of her head.

"I know it was a rocky journey," she continued, "but I personally wouldn't change a thing. And now,

I get to say that my best friend in the world is also my husband."

"Best friends forever takes on a whole new meaning now, huh?" Gabe teased.

"You know it," Elise replied, giggling.

"Well, wife," Gabe said, kissing her long and slow. "We should probably stop playing hooky and get back to our reception, what do you say?"

Elise kissed him back. "I say, let's hit the dance floor!"

Gabe laughed, pulling her back down the sidewalk and back into Brady's Bar. As they rejoined the crowd of family and friends inside and began dancing, Elise looked around. Everyone she loved most in the world was gathered in this room, her best friend and now husband was by her side, and she was a married woman. Joy bubbled up inside her, and she threw her head back and laughed from the sheer happiness of it all.

"What's so funny?" Gabe asked.

"Nothing," she replied, beaming up at him. "It's just that today is the best day."

"The best day so far," he countered. "I plan to make each day better than the last, so you'd better get ready."

She grinned, leaning against his arm. "I can't say I haven't been warned!"

The future looked very bright indeed.

Thank you for reading the *Sea Breeze Cove* series! For more uplifting, small-town women's fiction with a splash of clean romance, dive into *Whale Harbor Dreams*, book one of the *Saltwater Sunsets* series. If you enjoyed this series, I think you'll love that one!

ALSO BY FIONA BAKER

The Marigold Island Series

The Beachside Inn

Beachside Beginnings

Beachside Promises

Beachside Secrets

Beachside Memories

Beachside Weddings

Beachside Holidays

Beachside Treasures

The Sea Breeze Cove Series

The House by the Shore

A Season of Second Chances

A Secret in the Tides

The Promise of Forever

A Haven in the Cove

The Blessing of Tomorrow

A Memory of Moonlight

The Snowy Pine Ridge Series

The Christmas Lodge

Sweet Christmas Wish

Second Chance Christmas

Christmas at the Guest House

The Saltwater Sunsets Series

Whale Harbor Dreams

Whale Harbor Sisters

Whale Harbor Reunions

Whale Harbor Horizons

Whale Harbor Vows

Whale Harbor Starlight

Whale Harbor Adventures

Whale Harbor Blessings

For a full list of my books and series, visit my website at www.fionabakerauthor.com!

ABOUT THE AUTHOR

Fiona writes sweet, feel-good contemporary women's fiction and family sagas with a bit of romance.

She hopes her characters will start to feel like old friends as you follow them on their journeys of love, family, friendship, and new beginnings. Her heartwarming storylines and charming small-town beach settings are a particular favorite of readers.

When she's not writing, she loves eating good meals with friends, trying out new recipes, and finding the perfect glass of wine to pair them with. She lives on the East Coast with her husband and their two trouble-making dogs.

Follow her on her website, Facebook, or Bookbub.

Sign up to receive her newsletter, where you'll get free books, exclusive bonus content, and info on her new releases and sales!

Made in United States
North Haven, CT
02 June 2023

37260765R00150